"I still want yo[u] more than a[ny]..."

Justin rolled over and gazed down intently at Caroline as he spoke.

"I don't think I need to be assured of that at this moment," she murmured indulgently, loving the feel of his weight on her.

"No," he acknowledged heavily. "But you said you love me, and I—I don't want to lose you."

Although he had hardly reacted to her earlier outburst, she could now see that it mattered to him very much. If only he'd open up to her.

"Has knowing I don't want our child made you hate me?" he ground out suddenly, lost inside himself. "Children are such vulnerable creatures, you see," he murmured raggedly. He shuddered and laid his head against her breast. "I can't love, Caroline. I'm sorry."

CAROLE MORTIMER, one of our most popular—and prolific—English authors, began writing in the Harlequin Presents series in 1979. She now has more than forty top-selling romances to her credit and shows no signs whatever of running out of plot ideas. She writes strong traditional romances with a distinctly modern appeal, and her winning way with characters and romantic plot twists has earned her an enthusiastic audience worldwide.

Books by Carole Mortimer

HARLEQUIN PRESENTS

HARLEQUIN SIGNATURE EDITION

Don't miss any of our special offers. Write to us at the following address for information on our newest releases.

Harlequin Reader Service
901 Fuhrmann Blvd., P.O. Box 1397, Buffalo, NY 14240
Canadian address: P.O. Box 603,
Fort Erie, Ont. L2A 5X3

CAROLE MORTIMER

uncertain destiny

Harlequin Books

TORONTO • NEW YORK • LONDON
AMSTERDAM • PARIS • SYDNEY • HAMBURG
STOCKHOLM • ATHENS • TOKYO • MILAN

Harlequin Presents first edition August 1988
ISBN 0-373-11100-2

Original hardcover edition published in 1987
by Mills & Boon Limited

CHAPTER ONE

'YOU may be pregnant, Caroline,' her husband accepted coldly, 'but *we* certainly aren't. The child you're carrying is not mine!'

She stared at Justin as if he had gone insane. She had just told him the most wonderful news any wife could tell a husband, had been in a state of euphoria ever since she had gone to the doctor this afternoon and he had confirmed her suspicion that she was six weeks pregnant. She had wanted to tell Justin straight away, wanted to rush over to his office and tell him, but had known it wasn't the right place to break the news to him that he was about to become a father for the first time, deciding a candlelit dinner for the two of them at home would be a much more romantic background.

The candles still burnt on the table, the roses that adorned its centre still smelt as sweet, and she still wore the black gown she had chosen to reassure Justin that pregnant women could still look sexy.

And she couldn't believe Justin had said what she thought he had! He couldn't really have said that—could he?

But as she looked up at the coldness of his gaze, the arrogant tilt to his head, the grim set to his sculptured lips, she knew that he had.

Oh, she knew that they never discussed the possibility of having children, but even so——

'Justin——'

'You see, Caroline,' he continued dismissively, his voice deadly calm. 'I'm incapable of fathering a child, by you or any other woman.' He sipped his wine with slow deliberation, looking at her with questioningly raised brows.

She should faint, scream, anything but just sit here staring at him as if she had turned to stone. But she still couldn't believe Justin was denying their child. It had to be a joke, a sick joke—what else could it be? It certainly couldn't be the truth!

'Did you hear me, Caroline?' he bit out. 'I said——'

'Will you stop this.' Her voice was shrill. 'Just stop it, Justin. It isn't funny!'

'I didn't think so either,' he drawled, taking another sip of his wine. 'And I don't believe you saw me laughing.'

She gave a pained frown at his too-calm behaviour. 'Justin, is there a possibility you were drinking before you came home this evening?' His being uncharacteristically drunk was the only other explanation she could think of for his outrageous behaviour.

His expression became even colder, his chair pushed back forcefully as he stood up to switch on the main light with a single movement of one long, gracefully male hand. He towered over her ominously as she blinked dazedly in the sudden bright light. 'I wasn't aware that I had ever given you reason to believe I've become a secret drinker!' he rasped.

There had to be some explanation for the nightmare this evening had suddenly become—although from Justin's cold displeasure at the suggestion, she knew alcohol wasn't it.

'Justin, I'm having a child.' Her hands were tightly clasped together in her lap, her back very straight as she sat rigidly in the chair, and she knew she must have the look of a naughty schoolgirl facing chastisement. Her throat arched defensively as she looked up at Justin. 'Your child,' she added pointedly.

He was so tall and dark, as savagely handsome as any young girl dreamt her husband would be. Dark hair was brushed smoothly back from his face, a black eye-patch rakishly covering the blindness of his left eye, but his sighted eye was more than capable of glittering silver with anger or contempt—as it was doing now! The elegant black evening suit should have had the effect of taming him somewhat, but instead it did the opposite, emphasising his leashed power, giving him the appearance of a barely restrained savage being, restricted by civilisation.

Caroline had been as overwhelmed by him at their first meeting as most people seemed to be, had never ceased to be enthralled by the complex man he was. But this, this she just didn't—*couldn't*—understand!

He shook his head now, deadly calm, although

the coldness of his gaze spoke of a fiercer emotion. *'Not* my child,' he repeated softly.

'Justin, of course the baby is yours. Who else's would it be?' she said exasperatedly.

His brows rose again. 'Tony's, perhaps?' he suggested mildly.

Her face paled. Dear God, he couldn't possibly believe what he was saying!

Justin moved to pour himself a glass of brandy from the decanter in the drinks cabinet. 'I think you should have asked him to share all this with you.' He drank down the brandy as he swept an arm in the direction of the romantic dinner she had planned so eagerly, and her own appearance with her red hair swept loosely on top of her head, her throat and shoulders left temptingly bare by the style of her black gown. 'Although maybe *his* wife might have objected to that,' he bit out hardly before leaving the room in measured strides, the slamming of another door in the house seconds later telling her he had gone to his study.

Caroline had half risen to her feet as he turned to leave, but dropped back down into the chair as she realised from his flinty expression that nothing she said just now would stop him.

She leant forward to absently blow out the candles, staring unseeingly at the spiral of black smoke that trailed upwards as the acrid smell filled the air.

They should have been celebrating now, with the champagne she had asked Mrs Avery to put on ice until after she had spoken to Justin. Instead Justin had stormed out on her, and she was sitting here hardly daring to think of the fact that he had disclaimed paternity of their child.

Loving Justin hadn't been easy from the first, and even now they were married it hadn't got any easier. But she had never before wished she had never met him!

That first evening had started out well, too, but also ended abruptly . . .

'I see my dear sister has been out hunting again,' Tony drawled at her side.

Caroline gave him a puzzled frown before turning to the door of this private room in one of London's finest hotels where Tony's parents had chosen to celebrate their fortieth wedding anniversary.

Paula Hammond was one of the most beautiful women she had ever seen, tall and elegant, with midnight-black hair, and a figure that was perfectly complemented by the red gown she wore. At thirty-five, she had been married and divorced, taking full advantage of her freedom the last five years.

Caroline had seen the other woman with many men during the eight months she had known Tony, but never before with the man at her side tonight. She would have remembered if she had ever seen this man before. Any woman would.

His hair was as black as Paula's, severely styled, although that in no way detracted from his fascinating attraction. His face wasn't handsome, more ruggedly compelling, and the eye-patch 'he wore only added to his aura of power, his sighted eye flickering uninterestedly over the friends and relatives of the Shepherds who were gathered in the room. His mouth firmed with impatience before he turned to murmur something to the vivacious Paula. With her undoubted beauty and air of sensuality, Paula usually held her dates in complete thrall, but it didn't look as if this man were as easily seduced; Paula gazing up at him longingly as she obviously spoke to him imploringly.

Caroline turned away, finding the sight of this usually self-confident woman pleading for a man's attention, particularly that man, who didn't look as if he gave a damn whose feelings he hurt if he left now, as he obviously wanted to do, strangely unsettling.

Tony chuckled at her side. 'I think I'll have to have a word with Mum and Dad,' he drawled. 'Obviously they forgot to tell my big sister to beware of wolves!'

She turned back to the man at Paula's side, frowning a little. He was mesmerisingly attractive, and she was sure she was far from the first woman to think so, but he didn't look as if he were particularly interested in attracting women to him, his slight impatience of movement giving the impression he didn't care to exert himself for such a trivial reason. He certainly didn't seem like any of the self-centred wolves she had encountered in the past.

Before Tony. For the past eight months they had

dated exclusively. She had been looking for a man like Tony all of her twenty-three years, very handsome with his light brown hair and twinkling hazel-coloured eyes, his boyish charm captivating her from the first. She knew it was only a matter of time before he asked her to marry him. And her answer was going to be a heartfelt yes!

'I'm sure Paula is perfectly capable of taking care of herself,' she lightly chided Tony for his malicious relish concerning his sister. She had learnt early on in her relationship with Tony that although he and Paula loved each other they did like to score off each other. The thought of his sister's downfall obviously filled him with glee.

Tony shook his head. 'She's chosen the wrong man if she wants to do that. 'The Wolf' could gobble her up in one bite!' His eyes narrowed as his sister leant against the other man, her long fingernails moving coaxingly in the dark hair at his nape. 'And this wolf always walks alone.'

The Wolf? She had thought Tony meant the term as an explanation of the other man's behaviour, but this time he had made it sound as if it were the other man's name.

'The Wolf?' she prompted curiously, suddenly breathless as that silver gaze moved over her as derisively as it had the rest of the guests, before suddenly swinging back again, sweeping over her from the top of her fiery-red hair, over the delicacy of her heart-shaped face, down the length of her slender body in the blue gown that matched the colour of her eyes and somehow made her hair look redder than ever, the long length of her legs, to her tiny feet in navy blue sandals.

His gaze moved back up to Caroline's face, flushed and hot now, feeling more and more uncomfortable as he continued to watch her while Paula spoke to him so seductively. It was strangely erotic to realise that while Paula was so intent on enticing him into staying with husky promises—no doubt of how the evening would end!—his attention was focused completely on Caroline. She almost felt as if he had reached out and touched her.

' 'The Wolf'.' Tony nodded, turning away from the other couple disgustedly. 'Paula works for his law firm, de Wolfe and Partners, and he earnt his nickname by always going for the jugular,' he added drily. 'He always prosecutes, never defends, and he never loses.'

Caroline moistened her lips nervously, finding it impossible to look away from that silver gaze. 'Never?' she breathed huskily, feeling her hands begin to shake as she held her glass of wine tightly to her.

'Nope,' Tony confirmed admiringly. 'I wonder how Paula managed to persuade him into coming here tonight; it's a sure fact it's the last place he wants to be,' he derided as Paula still exerted all the charm on the other man of which she was capable—all to no avail, by the way he glanced at her so mockingly.

Caroline took advantage of his brief shift of attention to turn away from him, feeling almost weak with relief at being free from him at last.

She had felt like a prisoner while he gazed at her so compellingly, and she didn't like the way she still trembled slightly even though she no longer looked at him. He exuded a sexuality that was primitive in its demand, and for a few brief minutes he had been demanding that she be completely aware of him. His appeal was raw, savage, and yet she hadn't been able to break free of it until he allowed her to. She didn't know what was the matter with her; she loved Tony, wanted to marry him, and yet just a look from a complete stranger had affected her more deeply than anything else she had ever known.

'—so for God's sake don't call him it to his face,' Tony was muttering.

She shook off the unsettling feelings Paula's date for the evening exerted on her. 'Sorry?' She gave Tony a questioning smile.

He met her smile warmly, glancing behind her. 'I said de Wolfe is only called 'The Wolf' behind his back,' he murmured hastily. 'Whatever you do, don't call him it!' He rolled his eyes expressively.

She frowned. 'But——'

'Tony,' Paula greeted him in her huskily attractive voice that, coupled with her sensual beauty, gave a false impression of a woman interested only in her appearance and what it could get for her. Paula Hammond was one of the most intelligent, shrewd women Caroline had ever met, which made her uncharacteristically kittenish behaviour around the man called de Wolfe all the more unnerving.

'Sis.' Tony moved slightly to kiss his sister on one creamy smooth cheek.

Irritation flashed in dark green eyes as Tony deliberately provoked her with a term he knew she disliked. The anger in her gaze promised him retribution later on.

But the anger faded to be replaced by warm seduction as she gazed up at the man at her side. 'Justin, I want you to meet my brother, Tony.' She scowled at her brother impatiently. 'And his girlfriend, Caroline Maxwell.' Her smile returned warmly as she looked at Caroline. 'This is Justin de Wolfe,' she announced a little triumphantly, her hand firmly on the crook of his arm, resting possessively on the expensive material of the black evening suit.

Caroline watched as the two men shook hands, her palms feeling damp as Justin de Wolfe turned to her, her breathing suddenly constricted. It was ridiculous, the foolishness completely unlike her, and yet she had a feeling that if Justin de Wolfe should touch her even once, she wouldn't want him to stop!

She gazed at him apprehensively, feeling panicked, knowing by the mocking twist to his firm mouth that her emotions were clearly readable to him. She drew in a controlling breath, holding out her hand politely, knowing she had no choice when he arched his dark brow at her so derisively.

As his long fingers closed over her much smaller ones she felt as if he took possession of her, warmth moving like quicksilver up her arm to rapidly engulf her whole body. She could scarcely breathe, filled with a painful ache she had never known before. And to break the contact was impossible.

His gaze narrowed, his head going back challengingly as he too seemed to feel the electricity pulsing between them. 'Miss Maxwell,' he finally murmured in a throaty voice.

God, even his voice was compelling, containing a mesmerising quality that ensured everyone would listen to him, even though he only spoke softly.

This couldn't be happening to her. She was a sensible woman, a trained nurse who had been responsible for dozens of patients over the years; she didn't believe in love at first sight. Or even second sight. Love to her was something that grew from mutual respect and interests, as she and Tony had, he a doctor, she a nurse. She didn't know anything about Justin de Wolfe except that he was lethal in a courtroom, was immune to any amount of female persuasion—and that he was dangerous! And the last was all she really needed to know about him.

'Mr de Wolfe.' She determinedly extracted her hand from within his suddenly steely grip.

'Would you care to dance, Miss Maxwell?' he prompted as the small band began to play a waltz.

Her panicked gaze flew up to meet his. She was tiny, only two inches over five feet, and he was at least a foot taller; if he held her in his arms her head would be on a level with his heart. And she didn't want to be anywhere near his heart! She didn't want to be anywhere near *him*.

'I——'

He didn't give her a chance to refuse him, his hand firm against her back as he guided her on to the small dance floor, maintaining that contact as he took her hand in his and began to move fluidly among the other couples dancing.

Sexual attraction, that was what this was. What else could it be that she felt hot and cold at the same time, barely knew what she was doing as he moved her expertly around the floor? And if she felt this way about a complete stranger, a man who seemed to distance himself from everyone and everything, then she had no business believing she should marry Tony if he should ask her.

'Relax,' Justin murmured into her hair, having gathered her close against his chest long ago.

How could she relax when her whole comfortably safe world was crumbling about her ears? She wanted to run from here and never have to see Justin de Wolfe again!

He moved back slightly to look down at her, very rakish with that black eye-patch over his left eye. 'Difficult to relax when you're burning up with desire, isn't it?' he mused drily.

Caroline gasped at the statement, about to deny it, when he suddenly drew her even closer against him, making her fully aware of his own desire for her.

'That's right,' he drawled self-derisively. 'I feel it, too.'

Felt what, too? This was utter madness. He was Paula's date for the evening; she had been seeing Tony for over eight months now. Whatever she and Justin de Wolfe felt for each other, it wasn't real, was based on mere sexual fantasy.

If only he didn't feel so very real as he moulded her so snugly against him that she could feel every muscle in his body!

'Are you and Shepherd sleeping together?' he suddenly asked.

Her eyes glittered deeply blue as she glared up at him. 'If you're trying to be insulting——'

His brows arched. 'I'm not. I just wanted to know how difficult it's going to be for you to finish with him.'

She drew in a ragged breath. 'As I have no intention——'

'Caroline,' he cut in patiently, as if he were reasoning with a rebellious child. 'We want each other. We're going to have each other. Often,' he stated with casual indifference. 'But I don't intend sharing you with Shepherd. Maybe it's old-fashioned of me, but when I'm involved with a woman I like to be the only man in her life. I *will* be the only man in your life.'

She looked about them frantically, sure Paula had allowed a certifiable maniac to walk off with her. She finally caught sight of Tony, he and Paula having what appeared to be one of their not unusual arguments, engrossed in each other and not in what was going on between herself and

Justin across the room. Fond of Tony as she was, she couldn't help wishing that he hadn't felt in an argumentative mood tonight. She needed rescuing, and from the way Justin's arms had tightened about her she didn't think she was going to be able to do it alone.

'I realise you're too young for me——'

'Couldn't it be that you're too old for me?' she gasped defensively, her cheeks aflame with heated colour as he looked down at her mockingly for her outburst. It was rather stupid to be reacting this way when the least objection to their ever seeing each other again was the fact that he was at least twelve years older than she was! There were far too many other reasons why they should never meet again.

He gave a derisive inclination of his head. 'I realise I'm too old for you,' he amended in a drily derisive voice. 'That we don't know a great deal about each other yet——'

'We don't know anything about each other,' she denied heatedly.

'We know that we could go to my apartment right now and not come out of the bedroom for a week,' he drawled confidently. 'And then it would only be because we would need to eat a little to get us through the next week!' His gaze was suddenly intense on her flushed face as she gazed up at him unprotestingly. 'I want to make love to you in every way possible,' he told her compellingly. 'In ways no one else has ever made love before.' A fire burnt deep in the depth of silver-grey, primitively savage.

Caroline swallowed hard, too weakened by his verbal lovemaking to be able to move away from him. 'And then what?' Her voice was husky.

His mouth twisted into the semblance of a smile. 'And then we start all over again!'

She shook her head at the eroticism he portrayed. 'But—but we don't know each other, don't *love* each other!'

'Love!' he scorned impatiently. 'Love is a vastly over-rated emotion that brings nothing but pain to those who suffer from it,' he dismissed abruptly. 'Do you have any idea how many people I've helped send to prison because of this so-called love?' He shook his head. 'Of course I don't love you, Caroline—— By the way that's going to be shortened to Caro whenever I want to make love to you,' he announced arrogantly.

'And I suppose you'll expect me to crawl into your bed to await your pleasure at those times?' she returned angrily. How dared he think he could just walk up to her and take over her life!

His mouth twisted. 'You overestimate my control where you're concerned, Caroline.' He deliberately emphasised the full use of her name. 'I expect us to make love wherever we happen to be at the time. It's all going to be part of the excitement. And you excite me as no other woman has,' he added intensely. 'And I can also assure you that the pleasure won't all be mine,' he finished, answering her angry taunt.

She knew that, already felt fevered with a need

she didn't want but didn't seem able to fight. But he couldn't seriously expect her to meekly leap into an affair with him.

She looked up at him searchingly, at the pulse that beat in his tightly clenched jaw, at the determination in his gaze, acknowledging the aura of power he had that told her he never said anything he didn't mean. They had only met a short time ago, Justin didn't believe in love because he had seen too many people hurt and destroy in the name of that emotion, and yet he calmly expected her to put her life in his hands. The trouble was, with his closeness seducing her like this, it would be so easy to do!

'Do you know that they call you——'

'I'm well aware of what they call me,' he bit out harshly. 'And why,' he added dismissively. 'I'm good at what I do, Caroline, and I make no apology for it. If a person breaks the law they should be punished for it.'

She swallowed hard at the cold implacability of his voice. 'Can you always be so sure they're guilty?'

'I wouldn't take the case if I weren't sure of that,' he dismissed confidently.

Caroline shivered at his calm certainty in his beliefs; she would hate to be at the receiving end of his wrath. She drew in a shaky breath. 'Tony said you're a wolf that always walks alone——'

'That isn't going to change just because we're having an affair,' he cut in firmly. 'I'm not accustomed to being answerable to anyone for my actions; I relish my privacy too much for that. We'll continue to maintain separate households during our relationship, but don't expect to spend too much time in yours,' he added drily, frowning suddenly. 'You know, I didn't want to come to this party with Paula tonight, even less so once I realised it was a family occasion, but as soon as I saw you I knew why I'd come against all my better judgment. I don't believe in love——' his mouth twisted '—but even I can't fight destiny.'

She, too, felt as if she were trying to fight something she had no power over. Justin called it destiny, but she was very much aware that this destiny could prove to be as much her destruction as her future happiness. And at the moment she wasn't sure which Justin was in her life although, knowing of the contempt with which he held love, she had a very good idea!

She pulled out of his arms. 'I was also destined to meet Tony,' she reminded him firmly. 'And I'm going to marry him.' She dared Justin to deny that.

He didn't. 'I'll take you back to him,' he drawled pleasantly, his hand light on her elbow.

Caroline trusted this calm friendliness even less than she did his blunt announcement that they were going to have an affair, eyeing him warily as they rejoined Tony and Paula, the brother and sister standing together in stony silence.

'You were gone long enough,' Tony snapped with uncharacteristic bad humour. 'I was almost desperate enough to ask Paula to dance!'

His sister gave him a disparaging look. 'Don't

delude yourself into thinking I would have accepted,' she scorned.

Hazel eyes flashed. 'I suppose you intend leaving now that you've done your duty by the parents?' he accused angrily.

Paula flushed guiltily. 'Justin and I have somewhere else to go,' she defended.

'I'm sure you do,' Tony acknowledged disgustedly.

It was obvious that Paula's intention of leaving only twenty minutes after her arrival was the reason she and Tony had been arguing all the time she and Justin were dancing. Caroline suddenly found, to her dismay, that she was as disgusted as Tony at the thought of the other couple leaving so that they could make love—but for completely different reasons.

She looked up at Justin uncertainly as he squeezed her arm reassuringly.

'Caro.'

It was the softest of murmurs, barely perceptible as he spoke close to her ear so that the other couple shouldn't hear him, and yet it was enough to reassure her that he didn't intend making love to Paula tonight, that it was her he wanted.

It was ridiculous to be pleased by the realisation, disloyal when she intended marrying Tony if he should ask her. But for that heart-stopping moment she wanted to be the one to leave with Justin, wanted to hear him murmur that shortened version of her name, that no one else had ever used before, over and over again as he made love to her.

'Why don't you stay on at the party, Paula?' Justin suggested briskly. 'I really do have to leave now.'

Paula looked alarmed as it seemed he would slip away from her. 'Oh, but——'

'I did warn you I didn't really have the time for a party tonight,' he cut in in a voice that brooked no further protest to his decision to leave, alone. 'I'll see you on Monday. Tony,' he nodded abruptly to the other man. 'Caroline,' he added lingeringly, his gaze holding her captive before he turned and strode purposefully across the room.

'Damn, damn, *damn!*' Paula muttered furiously as Justin left without a backwards glance.

'You caught yourself the wrong one this time, sister dear,' Tony taunted.

Paula answered as heatedly as Tony had known she would, but Caroline wasn't listening to their conversation, still staring across the room to where Justin had left seconds earlier. He hadn't said anything about seeing her again but she knew that he was arrogant enough to try to contact her again, that he hadn't given up.

The rest of the evening was an anti-climax for Caroline, who barely noticed that Tony and Paula seemed to argue most of the time. Considering they were two mature people, Tony thirty to Paula's thirty-five, both in exacting professions, Tony a doctor while Paula was a very competent lawyer, the two of them seemed to revert to the nursery whenever they were together like this!

Caroline felt completely drained by the time the

party drew to a close, finding it extremely difficult to behave as if that disturbing conversation with Justin de Wolfe had never taken place, and finding it even more difficult to behave as if nothing had changed between herself and Tony.

But it had changed; nothing was the same, not even her response to his goodnight kisses once they reached her flat.

'You're tired.' Tony finally drew back at her lack of enthusiasm for his caresses. 'I'll see you tomorrow after work.'

Of course she was tired; it had been a long and traumatic day on the ward. Everything would look different after a good night's sleep. Most of all that conversation with Justin de Wolfe. She firmly put from her mind the fact that tiredness had never made her unresponsive towards Tony before.

But once she was in bed the memory of Justin de Wolfe and his outrageous suggestion that they had an affair wouldn't be put from her mind any longer. He was such a fascinating man, his elusiveness where women were concerned making him more so, she admitted that. And he wanted her. He hadn't said that he loved her, or that he even liked her, but he did want her.

And she didn't for one moment believe his calm acceptance of her refusal to see him again was the end of it, also knew that a little thing like not knowing her address wouldn't stop a man like him if he were really determined to see her again. And he had seemed very determined.

She——

***

'Caroline.'

She turned to the doorway, her eyes wide, shaking slightly as she saw from the cold expression on Justin's face that he was still filled with that implacable anger.

His expression darkened as she eyed him apprehensively. 'You're tired, and it's late,' he bit out, striding purposefully across the room, standing so close to her chair that the heat of his body reached out and touched her. 'It's time we were both in bed.'

'But the things you said,' she reminded in a pained voice. 'The baby——'

'I don't think anything can be gained by discussing that any more tonight.' His gaze was cold, his mouth a taut line as he pulled her effortlessly to her feet.

'But——'

'Let's go to bed, Caroline,' he prompted impatiently. 'Perhaps things will look—different, in the morning,' he added in a hard voice.

If they went to bed together tonight, would he want to make love to her? He was furious at the idea of the child she carried, but the flame she could see in the depths of his gaze told her it hadn't changed his desire for her.

But nothing would have changed in the morning; she would still be pregnant and, from the hardness of his expression, Justin would still be denying the child was his.

She shook her head, several tendrils of fiery hair

escaping the loose upsweep on to the crown of her head. 'The baby isn't going to disappear overnight,' she told him.

'Are you refusing to share a bed with me, Caroline?' He spoke softly.

She never had, not from the beginning, unable to fight the truth of his claim at their first meeting. They always wanted each other to the point of desperation; just a look from her or the murmur of her name from Justin and the two of them would be making love. It had been that way since she first went out with him.

But they couldn't make love tonight, not with the baby's existence standing so solidly between them. She would never be able to forget that Justin had accused her of carrying Tony's child; not even the mindless pleasure she could always find in Justin's arms could make her forget that.

She heaved a ragged sigh. 'I have to, Justin,' she told him emotionally. 'We have to settle the matter of the baby before I——'

He stiffened, and suddenly Caroline had a feeling much like a person in a courtroom must do just before Justin began to cross-examine them.

'The matter is settled, Caroline,' he bit out. 'The child inside you is not mine. It is a medical impossibility for it to be so.'

'But——'

'Medically impossible, Caroline,' he repeated harshly.

'Doctors make mistakes——'

'Not this time.' His voice was a cold rasp.

'But they have to have done,' she insisted desperately. 'I was a virgin that first night we were together, you know that!' She looked up at him appealingly.

He gave an acknowledging inclination of his head. 'But you did insist on seeing Tony—alone—after that, to explain that you intended marrying me,' he reminded her calmly.

Caroline felt the colour leave her cheeks, staring at him as if she couldn't believe what he was suggesting. 'Justin, you can't think, believe——'

'What other explanation can there be for your pregnancy?' He shrugged dismissively.

'You prefer to believe I went to bed with Tony just before we were married rather than that the doctor who told you you're sterile made a mistake?' she gasped in a pained voice.

His gaze was narrowed. 'Yes.'

She sat down suddenly. 'Then you're right, discussing this any further wouldn't help at all,' she said dully, blinking back the tears.

He nodded abruptly. 'I'll sleep in the spare bedroom tonight,' he told her harshly. 'We'll have to decide tomorrow what's to be done about the baby.'

That roused her from the sea of pain she had been drowning in. 'What's to be done?' she repeated slowly, reluctantly, watching him warily.

'I don't want children, Caroline,' he stated abruptly. 'I never have.'

What did that mean? That he wanted her to leave and take the baby with her, or that he just *didn't want the baby?*

CHAPTER TWO

CAROLINE awoke with a groan, pushing the hair out of her face as she rolled over to look at the bedside clock. Nine-thirty; Justin would already have left for the day.

She sat up in the bed, staring down at her still-flat stomach, already feeling an affinity with the child that nestled inside her.

How could Justin deny that child, refuse to even acknowledge its existence other than as an unwelcome intrusion into their marriage?

When she had pressed him last night to explain exactly what he meant by his remark about 'not wanting children', he had told her he thought it would be better if they slept on it and came to a decision in the morning. She hadn't wanted to wait until then, had demanded he answer her. He had completely withdrawn from her then, leaving her standing beside the table that was still set for their celebration, and when she had desperately followed him up the stairs it was to find the spare bedroom door locked against her.

He couldn't mean for her to choose between him or their baby, could he? Even if he didn't believe it was his child, he couldn't really expect her to—no! She wouldn't even acknowledge him demanding that possibility. To her it *wasn't* a possibility.

She had to persuade him to see another doctor, knowing beyond a shadow of doubt that the child she carried was Justin's. There had been no one else for her, not before or since him. How could there have been, when he fulfilled her completely, possessed her like a drug that made her body feverish and her senses so attuned to him that the mere sight of him drove her wild with need?

Their first night together, here in this very house, she had submitted herself to a far greater power than any she possessed, had known herself lost from Justin's first caress . . .

Even Caroline hadn't been prepared for his call the night they met. She was on the point of going to bed shortly after Tony had left when the telephone began to ring. Envisaging another unexpected night on duty when one of the night-staff had let them down, she picked the receiver up with a groan.

'So you and Shepherd *don't* sleep together,' came the husky greeting.

Caroline stiffened, instantly alert, moistening suddenly dry lips. 'Justin?' she said uncertainly.

'Unless some other man questioned you tonight about your relationship with Shepherd,' he acknowledged drily.

She gave an irritated frown; she had expected to hear from him, but this! 'I don't know anyone else that arrogant,' she admitted abruptly, somehow knowing that amusement had darkened his gaze.

'How did you get my number?' she prompted waspishly.

'I telephoned Paula first and asked her,' he revealed calmly.

'You——' She gasped, closing her eyes as she imagined what the other woman had made of that, the answer not a pleasant one.

'Would you like to add "bastard" after the "arrogant"?' he mused.

'Yes!' she snapped. 'And how do you know Tony isn't waiting in the bedroom for me right now?' she demanded angrily.

'Paula was only too eager to tell me that you and her brother don't sleep together,' Justin mocked. 'I believe she imagined it would deter my interest.'

Caroline gripped the receiver tightly, ashamed of how much she hoped that hadn't happened. 'And did it?' She waited breathlessly for his answer.

'Not in the least,' he answered confidently. 'I like a woman who can be a little choosy about who she goes to bed with.'

Did he also like a woman who hadn't been to bed with anyone? she wondered a little dazedly. Really, the man had no scruples at all, telephoning her in this way!

'How do you know that choice will include you?' she snapped, annoyed at the awkward situation he had put her in with Tony and his sister.

'Are you saying it doesn't?' His voice had gone huskily soft.

She didn't even know why she was having this conversation with him! He wasn't her type at all, was too worldly, too sophisticated, too experienced when it came to women. He had known exactly how to pique her interest tonight, to keep her dangling there until he decided to draw her into his web of sensuality.

'Caro?' he prompted gruffly.

Oh, God, just the sound of her name on his lips caused a shiver of awareness down her spine!

'All right,' he chuckled softly at her dazed silence. 'I don't find making love over the telephone very satisfying either. Dinner tomorrow?'

By tacit agreement she and Tony hadn't seen anyone but each other the last eight months, and no words of a permanent relationship had been mentioned between them, yet she knew it was an accepted thing between them.

She wasn't about to jeopardise her relationship with Tony just because of a mad attraction for Justin de Wolfe!

'I'll only keep asking, Caroline.' Justin seemed to realise she was about to say no; his voice was hard. 'And if Tony told you anything about me at all you have to know I never give up when I want something as badly as I seem to want you.'

Tony hadn't exactly said that, but he had told her this man never lost, which amounted to the same thing!

'Look, Caroline, if my honesty in admitting I want to make love to you is too much for you to accept, then I'm sorry,' he said impatiently at her continued silence. 'But I stopped going out on platonic dates years ago. And if you think I make a habit of picking up women at parties you would be wrong about that, too,' he added in a hard voice. 'My libido is as strong as any other man's,' he admitted derisively, 'but I rarely have the time to indulge it. Now will you have dinner with me tomorrow night?'

She had a feeling that when this man did rouse himself enough to show a preference for a particular woman he never received a lukewarm response, let alone faced the possibility of being turned down. As he was about to be!

'I'm busy tomorrow night,' she told him dismissively.

'Caro——'

'I said no, Mr de Wolfe,' she refused firmly as the silky caress of his voice threatened to once again seduce her.

'I meant it when I said I would keep asking, Caroline,' he warned grimly. 'I can't take no for an answer from you.'

Her hand shook as she slowly replaced the receiver, half expecting him to ring straight back, but realising when he didn't do so that he was wise enough to know that would just make her even angrier.

When she met Tony the next night she knew Paula had lost no time in telling her brother of Justin's interest. It didn't seem to matter to Tony that she had refused to see the other man. He was furious that Justin de Wolfe had asked her out at all, seemed to think she must have encouraged the other man in some way—Justin de Wolfe, reputedly not a man to exert himself for any woman.

But he seemed determined to do so for her, turning up at the most unexpected times during the next three weeks, meeting her as she came off duty, calling around at the flat, and always with the purpose of repeating his dinner invitation.

Much as she hated to admit it, this show of attention from a man who rarely bothered with women at all began to affect her, and in a strange way she began to look forward to seeing him, the sexual tension between them building each time she did so. Ultimately it affected her relationship with Tony; she was no longer at ease in his company as he seemed to regard her suspiciously. Finally he lost his temper completely and told her he thought they should stop seeing each other, that she should go out with Justin de Wolfe and see how fascinating she found him when he left her after a few dates!

She hadn't thought Tony could mean what he had said, expecting him to come round and apologise, but after three days of waiting she realised he had meant every word. Her hurt turned to anger, and the next time Justin asked her out she accepted.

When she opened the door to him at seven-thirty that evening she knew she had made a mistake. Tonight even the veneer of civilisation had been stripped from him, the black evening suit and snowy white shirt doing nothing to disguise his primitive savagery. Any idea she might have had about just being another conquest to him was wiped out as she met the blazing desire in his gaze; Justin was a man who usually held himself in cool control, and he no more welcomed this feeling of helplessness to desire than she did. He just knew it was useless to fight the inevitable.

Being taken into his arms was inevitable, too. Her throat arched as Justin's mouth came down firmly on hers, both of them exploding with a need that had barely been held in check since the moment their gazes first met.

She could taste him, feel him along every nerve-ending in her body, knew that Justin's veneer of sophistication had slipped because he was just as unnerved by this desire.

He kissed her deeply, hotly, his hands moving over her body with fevered insistence, cupping one pert breast to caress the pulsing nub with fiery rhythm.

Her hands were tangled in the dark thickness of his hair as she clung to him, her body on fire, knowing that if he hadn't held her so tightly she would have fallen to the carpeted floor.

Finally he drew back with a ragged sigh, resting his forehead on hers. 'Hello,' he greeted her belatedly.

She gave a shaky laugh, her hands still clinging to his broad shoulders. 'I dread to think what you could do with "Hello, darling"!'

He shook his head to clear it of the sexual haze. 'I have no doubt we'll find out,' he said gruffly.

'Are you ready to go?'

The question held much more than its surface significance, at least, for her, but one look into his arrogantly assured face when he arrived and she had known she was more than ready, that she had probably been waiting for tonight all her life. Her relief that she had waited, and not fallen into that trap a lot of her friends had by sleeping with men they were merely fond of, was immense. She knew with certainty that somehow during the last three weeks—probably instantly she saw him—she had fallen in love with this enigmatic man, that she had been fighting a losing battle.

'I'm ready,' she nodded, smiling shyly, knowing her mouth had to be bare of lipgloss by now, and not really caring. Justin was looking at her as if he would like to eat her, and her mouth felt swollen and red enough without the aid of artifice.

Later they were alone in his apartment, although Caroline doubted he had actually cooked the delicious meal they served up together. No doubt he had someone that came in to cook and clean for him, her presence unobtrusive in the extreme; Justin didn't give the impression of a man who hurried home at the end of the day to spend time cooking.

The food was deliciously prepared and cooked, smelt wonderful, too, and yet neither of them did justice to it. Caroline couldn't keep her eyes off Justin for more than a few seconds at a time, her anticipation high, and he seemed to be lost in brooding silence as he absently pushed the food around on his plate.

'I can't wait any longer!' He suddenly threw his fork down, pushing his plate away to stand up. 'Caro, I *need* to make love to you. Very badly.'

She could see just how badly by the fevered glitter of his gaze, his hands clenched at his sides. And if she were honest—and that seemed to be what Justin demanded of her—she couldn't wait any longer, either.

She stood up, too, her legs a little shaky, and then they were in each others arms, and it was just as if there had been no break from their earlier impassioned kisses, Justin's mouth wide and moist against hers, his tongue moving into her fiercely at the same time as he pulled her thighs high against him.

He was hard and pulsating against her, groaning low in his throat at the satiny feel of her thighs, his kisses becoming even fiercer, devouring, filled with hunger as he began to pull off her clothes.

Caroline felt a shiver as the cool air caressed her body as her gown fell at her feet, the feel of Justin's dinner jacket abrasive against her naked breasts, rubbing against the tips, filling her lower body with a warm ache that flamed moistly as Justin touched her there.

He suckled on her breast, drawing it hungrily into his mouth, the pleasure-pain causing her to whimper low in her throat, breathing shakily, her back arched as she pushed herself against him.

He drew just as fiercely on the other nipple while his hand cupped and caressed the breast he had abandoned, holding her up against him as if she weighed nothing at all.

She couldn't stand it any more, needing more, needing it all, pushing frantically at his jacket, their mouths fused together as Justin helped her with the removal of his clothes, sinking down on to the floor with her, lying between her parted thighs as he moved restlessly against her.

She cradled either side of his face as their kisses went on and on, moist and hungry, fevered, Caroline arching against him as he continued to caress her aching breasts.

His legs felt abrasive against her as he moved above her, increasing her passion, the ache between her thighs becoming almost a pain.

And then he came into her, slowly, not forcefully, easing her sudden tension, gently penetrating the barrier that parted and finally moved aside altogether. There should have been pain, but there wasn't, only an unfamiliar feeling of fullness, a slight discomfort that made her muscles contract at the intrusion.

And then Justin began to move within her, gently stroking her, the heat instantly returning, consuming, until her breath was coming in strangled gasps, her head thrashing from side to side as she knew she was about to shatter, to be devoured by the burning ache that filled her whole body now.

Suddenly her back arched, her thighs thrust fiercely against Justin, her eyes wide with wonder on Justin's face as the pleasure exploded, imploding in a million different places in her body.

Justin continued to thrust against her, and as one wave of pleasure ended another began, until she felt it would never stop, awestruck as she watched the savage beauty of Justin's face as he grimaced as though in pain, groaning loudly, suddenly even more fierce against her, driving her over the edge again as she felt his own fevered release.

He gently lowered his weight against her, burying his face in her perfumed hair, his breath deep and rasping. 'It was more,' he finally groaned, 'so much more than I even imagined!'

She could never have imagined anything as devastatingly shattering as the passion they had just shared. She didn't need to be experienced to know that it had been something special. She hadn't known whether she would be able to feel pleasure at all the first time they made love, but it had been never-ending, and even now she wanted him again. As she felt him stir against her she knew that it was what he wanted, to.

He looked down at her questioningly as his passion rekindled. 'Are you all right?' His voice was husky.

A delicate blush darkened her cheeks. 'I don't hurt at all,' she assured him softly, finding her shyness utterly ridiculous considering the intimacy of their positions.

He frowned. 'You'll probably be a little sore tomorrow,' he warned sympathetically. 'But as long as you feel OK now?' Still he hesitated about repeating that fiery splendour.

'I feel fine,' she said gruffly. 'I feel better than fine,' she added determinedly. 'And I want you again, too.'

He smiled his satisfaction with her answer, and it made him look more rakish than ever, his hair tousled, the eye-patch giving him a devilish look.

She tentatively touched his cheek near the black patch. 'What happened?' She frowned her concern.

'A dissatisfied client,' he dismissed shruggingly, bending to move his lips against her throat.

Her frown deepened, even though his lips sent a delicious thrill down the length of her spine. 'I thought you always won?'

'Not *my* dissatisfied client,' Justin gently mocked. 'I made sure he was put away.'

Her fingers stilled against his cheek. 'But if he was put in prison . . .'

'They all get out eventually,' Justin explained tautly. 'I do my job, Caroline,' he added softly as she shivered in reaction. 'This man just happened to believe there was something personal in my prosecution of him. When he got out of prison he paid me a little visit.' He frowned.

She was still trembling. 'Where is he now?'

Justin's mouth twisted. 'Back in prison, for attacking me this time.' He shrugged dismissively. 'It really isn't important.'

'But he—he blinded you in one eye!' she gasped.

He nodded. 'And it isn't a pretty sight. But then

knife wounds never are,' he murmured almost to himself. 'But let's not talk about that now, Caroline.' His gaze moved over her hungrily. 'I want to make love to you again. And this time we might even make it as far as the bedroom,' he added self-derisively.

Caroline blushed as she looked around them and realised they were still in the dining-room.

Justin's mouth quirked. 'Don't look so embarrassed, Caro,' he teased throatily. 'At least it wasn't *on* the table!'

He carried her through to his bedroom, beginning to make love to her again, more slowly this time as neither of them were so feveredly desperate, but it was just as intense, just as shattering, the two of them lying damply together as their hands still moved caressingly over each other, unable to stop the touching.

As the night passed swiftly by, Justin was indefatigable, making love to her again and again, groaning his protest when she had to leave him in the morning to go to work.

He watched her as she dressed in the gown that seemed so out of place in the brightness of the sunny Sunday morning. After the intimacies they had shared it was a little ridiculous to feel shy in front of him, but the way he watched her so steadily unnerved her, and she heaved a silent sigh of relief as she zipped up the back of her gown.

'Can you be available on Thursday?' He sat back against the coffee-coloured pillows, his chest bare as the matching sheet lay draped across his thighs. He was so completely male, his body all hard muscle, and he knew how to use that body to the satisfaction of both of them. 'If not next Thursday——' he frowned at her silence '—it will have to wait a couple of weeks; I'm going to be very busy until then.'

Caroline suddenly realised what he had said, shaking her head to clear it of the sensual spell this man seemed to exert over her without even trying.

What did he mean, could she be available next Thursday, if not it would have to wait a couple of weeks? She knew she had behaved like a wanton the night before, but she had thought the passion more than returned; she didn't expect him to try and fit her in among all of his other social engagements now that he had taken what he seemed to want!

Her face paled as she realised what a fool she had been to imagine that what was between them was special. How many other women had told themselves the same thing, only to realise that what was love on their side was merely lust on the side of the man?

She was twenty-three years old and had received more than her fair share of sexual proposals over the years, mainly from medical students who believed a nurse was fair game, but she had behaved like a fool last night, had become totally infatuated with a man who saw taking a woman to bed as no more than another conquest he had to make.

A sob caught in her throat as she turned away to search for her shoes where she had placed them on the floor, tears blinding her. She stiffened as she felt Justin's nakedness behind her as he pulled her back against him.

'Don't you want to marry me?' His voice was silkily soft against her ear.

Marry? She turned slowly to face him, her eyes wide, searching the derisive amusement of his face. His derision seemed to be self-directed, as if he, too, found the prospect of marriage surprising, even if he were resigned to it.

'Destiny played a dirty trick on me three weeks ago,' he drawled ruefully. 'The moment I saw you I wanted you,' he told her calmly. 'And after only one night with you I know that no other woman has ever matched me in passion the way you do.'

She blinked, still dazed that he had meant he wanted to *marry* her next Thursday. 'You want to marry me because—because we make love well together?' she said disbelievingly, the tender ache in her body reminding her of the night that had just passed, of just how well they made love.

'Not the sort of marriage proposal you were ever expecting to hear, was it?' he mocked, cupping her chin to caress her cheek lightly with the pad of his thumb. 'But it isn't just how well your body fits to mine,' he said ruefully. 'It's because I know, realised as I waited for you the last three weeks, that I don't ever want any other man to have you. Even less so now.' His smile was gentle at her self-conscious blush at his reference to her virginity. 'No, I'm not in love with you,' he seemed to read the uncertain question in her eyes, 'I've already told you my opinion of that emotion,' he scorned. 'But I do know this wanting isn't going to go away in a hurry, that it probably never will, and that I want my claim on you to be a public one. Is that going to be enough for you?' He looked down at her steadily, his gaze narrowed to a silver slit.

Because she was too much in love with him to say no, it had to be enough.

They had been married four days later, Justin having no family of his own to invite, only her parents, her brother and sister—Simon and Sonia—and a couple of her friends in attendance. Until he met her Justin really had been a wolf that preferred to walk completely alone.

Almost seven weeks of marriage hadn't seen too many changes in her husband. When they made love they were completely attuned, but the rest of the time Justin chose to hold himself aloof, rarely talking about his work to her, only agreeing to socialise with her family because he knew she expected it of him.

And now he seemed to think she had conducted some sort of experiment with Tony in between his proposal and their wedding, to see if she and Justin really were so unique in their passion for each other, and that the baby she carried was the result of that experiment. She hadn't needed to make love with another man to be sure of that!

The baby she carried was Justin's, no matter what he believed about his being sterile. My God, why hadn't he told her he believed he could never give her children? It wouldn't have changed her decision to marry him, but he should have told her, damn it! What sort of man married a woman without telling her something as important as that? A man like Justin, she acknowledged dully. He didn't want children; why should he bother to explain that he could never give her any?

Dear God, where did they go from here? What were they going to 'decide' about the baby today?

She sat up straight against the pillows as a soft knock sounded on the door, and forced a tight smile to her lips as Mrs Avery put her head around the door, before entering with a bright smile as she saw Caroline was awake.

'Mr de Wolfe told me to let you sleep this morning.' She put a tray of coffee down on the bedside table. 'But I thought I heard you moving around a few minutes ago.'

Justin's 'unobtrusive' housekeeper had turned out to be this friendly little woman with warm blue eyes. She had confided in Caroline shortly after she moved in as Justin's wife that the Mrs part of her name was merely a cursory title, that she had never married but felt it was necessary to be a Mrs in the job she chose to do. Mrs Avery was almost sixty, and Caroline sincerely doubted that Justin would ever feel the inclination to chase her around the apartment, but if the other woman felt happier being thought a married woman then she wasn't about to spoil that for her. The two of them had become firm friends over the weeks, Mrs Avery treating Caroline just like the daughter she had never had. She had no doubt the housekeeper was going to be thrilled when she was told about the baby. But she dared not tell anyone about that yet, not until she had sorted things out with Justin. He had to be convinced that the baby was his!

'I have to be on duty in just over an hour.' She accepted the coffee gratefully.

Justin had been very amenable about her continuing with her career, although she had cut down on her hours slightly, knowing Justin wouldn't appreciate her working late into the evening or during the night. She couldn't help wondering now, a little bitterly, if he hadn't encouraged her to continue with her career because he had known she would never have children to occupy her time. Children of his, that was.

Bitter reproach on her part wasn't going to help this situation, she inwardly reproved. She had to try and look at this from Justin's point of view. For years he had believed himself sterile, had probably come to terms with that fact; of course he was going to find it difficult to believe now that she was carrying his child. Perhaps the hours he had spent alone in bed last night, the first time they had slept apart since their marriage, had given him a chance to think, to realise that a mistake just could have been made.

Yes, she was sure that by the time he got home this evening he would have realised she could never have made love with any other man but him, that the child had to be his. His decision that he didn't want children had probably been a defence mechanism because he didn't believe he could ever have any. By the time he got home this evening they would be able to discuss all this rationally.

Some of the despair left her as she went to work on that happier note, putting her troubles from her mind as for the rest of the day she concentrated on her patients.

She was going to miss her work on the wards once she had the baby. Being a nurse had been the only thing she had ever wanted to do, all her educational qualifications gained for just that reason. It had been a wonderful five years, but no doubt the baby would help compensate for what she lost. She wanted this baby so much, wanted to give Justin the son he had thought never to have.

He wasn't home when she got in, so she went through to have a soak in the bath before dinner, frowning her puzzlement when she returned to the bedroom an hour later to discover he still wasn't home.

He wasn't usually this late home. Unless——

She hurried out to the kitchen; Mrs Avery was just in the process of putting the finishing touches to dinner—for one. Whenever Justin was going to be late, or not going to make dinner at all, she had requested that the housekeeper serve her dinner on a tray rather than going to all the trouble to lay the table formally; Justin wasn't coming home for dinner tonight!

She moistened her suddenly dry lips as the housekeeper looked up at her curiously. Justin hadn't called her at work today as he usually did when he was going to be late or miss dinner, but it was obvious that he had let Mrs Avery know of his plans. How to find out what those plans were without making an absolute fool of herself!

She forced a tight smile to her lips. 'It's as well Justin isn't in for dinner tonight as we have steak pie,' she remarked lightly.

Mrs Avery smiled mischievously. 'Not one of his favourites, is it?' she acknowledged. 'But I know how you enjoy it, so as soon as Mr de Wolfe telephoned me this morning to say he would be away for a few days I decided to prepare all your favourite meals to cheer you up. No wonder you were looking a bit peaky this morning when I brought in your coffee. Such a pity he had to go away so soon after you were married. But I——'

Caroline was no longer listening as the woman chattered on. Justin had gone away for a few days. Was that the decision he had come to during the long night hours they had been apart, separated by the thickness of a wall? Were those 'few days' going to turn into a week, and then a month? Did he ever intend coming back?

CHAPTER THREE

CAROLINE still felt numb the next day, didn't know whether Justin expected her to leave during his absence or wait until he returned and told her to go.

Justin might have married her for all the wrong reasons, but she loved him very much, had hoped the desire he felt for her would eventually turn into love, too. The fact that he had gone away, without even bothering to call and tell her, seemed to say that he could never accept the child she carried as his, that he no longer wanted her because of it.

But if that were the way he felt, he was going to have to tell her that to her face, was actually going to have to tell her to leave. She didn't doubt that he was capable of it; she had realised as she lay awake for the second night in a row that she was no closer to him emotionally than she had been six weeks ago. She had come to know him, however, and if he still stubbornly believed her to be carrying another man's child, Tony's child, he wouldn't hesitate to end their marriage. Like someone expecting the axe to fall, she waited.

The last thing she needed later that morning was a visit from a friend of Justin's she had never met before and whom he had never mentioned.

In his mid-thirties, the same as Justin, Don Lindford seemed nice enough, but, with Caroline so worried about her relationship with Justin, he couldn't have called at a worse time!

He shook her hand politely. He was a couple of inches under six feet, good-looking in a pleasant sort of way, with his sandy-brown hair brushed neatly to one side, and warm brown eyes.

'I was sorry I missed the wedding,' he smiled. 'I was away at the time and couldn't make it.'

'That's all right.' She indicated he should sit down. 'I'm afraid Justin hasn't spoken of you,' she admitted awkwardly as they sat across from each other.

He chuckled softly. 'That sounds like old Justin,' he mused. 'We go back a long way, but Justin more than lives up to his reputation of being a lone wolf.'

'Yes,' she acknowledged dully, wondering if that was what Justin was considering going back to. It was a certainty he didn't think this 'cub' was his!

'I have to admit to being surprised when I heard he had married,' Don Lindford said ruefully. 'Although since I've met his bride for myself, perhaps it was understandable,' he added warmly.

'Only perhaps?' she teased, starting to relax in his company. Justin never had spoken about any of his friends, but she had known he must have made some over the years; this man came as a pleasant surprise. Somehow she had been expecting any friend of Justin's to be as arrogantly aloof as he usually was.

'Definitely understandable,' he grinned conspiratorially. 'Your housekeeper said she isn't expecting Justin back today?' He frowned.

Caroline drew in a ragged breath. 'No.'

He pulled a face. 'He's taking a chance leaving you alone so soon after the wedding. If it had been me I would have taken you with me on my business trip.'

She smiled her gratitude at the compliment, giving a rueful grimace. 'There are some occasions when a wife would just be in the way,' she excused evasively.

'Hm,' Don Lindford acknowledged thoughtfully. 'Oh, well.' He stood up. 'I won't keep you any longer. I just thought I'd drop in and say hello to Justin's bride once I learnt he wasn't available. It's been nice meeting you.'

'Caroline,' she encouraged, also standing up. 'Could I offer you a cup of tea or—or anything?' she said awkwardly.

'No, thanks,' he refused warmly. 'If you could just tell Justin I called, and that I'll be in touch again soon?'

'Of course.' She walked him to the door. 'I really am sorry he wasn't here, I'm sure the two of you have a lot to talk about as you haven't seen each other for some time.'

'Yes,' he nodded. 'Once again, it's been nice to have met you, Caroline.'

She closed the door once he had left, turning with a thoughtful smile. She had been beginning to wonder if Justin had any friends after six weeks and not a mention of one; Don Lindford wasn't half as awesome as she had imagined friends of Justin would be. She would have to get Justin to invite him over for dinner sometime.

If she was still here. Well, she wasn't leaving without a fight; of that she was certain.

It seemed to be her day for unexpected visitors, her sister Sonia calling that afternoon.

Caroline had spent most of the afternoon pretending an interest in the book she was currently reading, knowing that if she looked too forlorn Mrs Avery would only offer her sympathy, and that was the last thing she needed, feeling particularly tearful today. She was well aware of the fact that her emotionalism was due to her pregnancy, but that didn't make it any easier to cope with. And the last thing she wanted today of all days was a confrontation with her sister.

She stood up stiffly as her sister was shown into the room by Mrs Avery.

Three and a half years her junior, Sonia was nevertheless possessed of a self-confidence that precluded her feeling uncomfortable no matter what the circumstances. And despite the awkwardness between the two sisters the last month, Sonia crossed the lounge to kiss Caroline warmly on the cheek.

'I called the hospital and they told me it was one of your days off,' Sonia explained dismissively. 'You're looking very beautiful,' she complimented easily. 'Married life is just wonderful, isn't it?' Her own eyes sparkled with happiness as she sat down without being invited to do so, a tall, blue-eyed blonde who moved with all the natural grace and beauty that had made her such a highly successful model the last two years.

No one looking at the two of them would ever believe they were related, but then that wasn't surprising; Caroline was an adopted child who had been almost four when her 'mother' suddenly produced twins, a boy and a girl. No one could have been more surprised than her parents at this startling event, having been told years earlier they would never have children of their own. But the appearance of Simon and Sonia had proved them wrong, and with Sonia and Simon's charming effervescence it was impossible not to love them.

It seemed ironic that what had happened to Caroline's parents twenty years ago was now happening to her and Justin—only, unlike them, Justin refused to believe a miracle had happened.

Caroline gave a grimace at the way her sister attacked the awkwardness between them with her usual bluntness. 'How is Tony?' she asked drily.

'Doing very well considering I'm not the world's best housewife.' Sonia gave a grin as Caroline smiled acknowledgement of her lack of talent in the home. 'I would have fared much better married to someone rich like your Justin.' She shrugged light-heartedly. 'But even if I do say so myself I'm doing OK as a doctor's wife.'

It had come as a shock when, two weeks after her own wedding to Justin, Sonia and Tony had gone off together and quietly got married. Sonia had admitted later to being attracted to Tony from the first, although not for anything would she have poached on Caroline's boyfriend. But as soon as Caroline had shown that she was in love with Justin, Sonia had felt free to pursue Tony, and she had chased him mercilessly once she knew Caroline no longer wanted him. From the haste with which he had married her sister he hadn't needed much chasing! After all the bitterness he had shown towards Caroline in the weeks before they had broken up, she couldn't help feeling resentful towards him for the abrupt way *his* affections had changed.

It hadn't been an easy situation the last month, with Tony still obviously angry about the way she had married Justin so suddenly, and Caroline slightly disgusted with the haste in which he had married Sonia, so the two couples had been avoiding each other. It had been a very awkward situation for their parents, doubly so as they had always been a close family before this. From the determined glint in Sonia's eyes she had come here to try and make it like that again.

But it wasn't Caroline she should be speaking to. Tony being the one to do most of the avoiding, still very angry about a love that she hadn't been able to do anything about.

Perhaps she had been a little angry with Sonia, too, for the way in which she had run after Tony, but considering the state of her marriage to Justin that anger now seemed petty and unimportant. What did it matter that Sonia had married Tony when she could be about to lose Justin?

'I'm glad.' She gave a strained smile.

Sonia gave her a considering look. 'Are you? I got the impression a month ago that you would be pleased to see me fall flat on my face.'

Caroline frowned at this uncharacteristic attack by her sunny-natured sister.

'Forget I said that,' Sonia dismissed self-disgustedly. 'I can't believe I did say that.' She grimaced, her lovely face smooth and creamy. 'I came here to invite you and Justin over to dinner tomorrow night.' She arched questioning brows.

Caroline was still frowning over her sister's accusation. There had always been rivalry between the two of them, but she had always thought that was natural between two sisters. She certainly hadn't wished for the downfall of Sonia's marriage to Tony, no matter how stunned she had been by it at the time.

'Caroline?' Sonia prompted at her silence, uncertainty clouding the usually laughing blue eyes.

She focused on her sister with effort. 'What does Tony say about that?'

'It was his idea,' Sonia announced happily. 'I think I must have passed the wife-test and so he's now ready to forget all the—unpleasantness of the past.'

'Sonia, are you really happy with Tony?' she probed worriedly.

'Oh, yes,' her sister answered without hesitation. 'Of course, he was still in love with you when we got married—he was, Caroline,' she insisted at her pained gasp. 'But all that's changed now,' she said confidently. 'I wouldn't be making this invitation if it hadn't,' she admitted bluntly.

Sonia had to be wrong about Tony's feelings a month ago. Oh, he had been angry about her decision to marry Justin, had accused her of wanting the other man for his wealth, had hauled any number of other bitter assaults on her during their last conversation, most of them concerning Justin's feelings for *her*. He certainly hadn't been in love with her then, if he ever had been; only his pride had been hurt.

'Do say you'll come, Caroline,' Sonia prompted at her silence. 'Mummy and Daddy would be so pleased if we all patched up our differences.'

Caroline's expression softened as she thought of the two people she had always known as her parents, knowing they had continued to love her as their own even after Sonia and Simon were born. The mend in the rift between their two daughters would please them, she knew. But she was still troubled by what Sonia had said about Tony's feelings for her.

'Sonia, you're wrong about Tony and me,' she frowned. 'We had already finished before Justin and I went out together.'

Her sister nodded. 'Tony told me all about that. For a while he was convinved that if he hadn't lost his temper over what he thought was going on between you and Justin, you would never have gone out with him and then married him. But that isn't true, is it?' Sonia shrugged.

No, it wasn't true. Eventually, she knew she would have gone to Justin anyway, without Tony finishing with her. Looking back on that time now, she was surprised she had managed to hold out the three weeks that she had!

'Tony realises that now?' she said anxiously.

'I think his pride was hurt more than anything,' her sister nodded. 'But he wants to make amends now, told me to invite you and Justin over for dinner.'

Her mouth twisted. 'Sure he doesn't just want to gloat about the success he's made of his marriage?'

'Maybe a little,' Sonia conceded, mischief lighting her eyes. 'But as you and Justin are so happy together, too, it doesn't really matter, does it?'

Caroline's humour left her as abruptly as it had appeared, a shadow darkening her eyes. She wasn't even sure she had a marriage any more.

Sonia was instantly attuned to her unhappiness. 'Everything is all right between you and Justin, isn't it?' She frowned her concern.

A lot of women, in the same circumstances, might worry that she would try to play upon Tony's past affection for her if her marriage was shaky, but Sonia wasn't like that, genuinely concerned for Caroline's happiness.

'Fine,' Caroline evaded; she wasn't ready yet to talk to anyone about the strain that existed between her and Justin. 'I'll have to talk to him first before making any arrangements to come over for dinner,' she thankfully excused. 'But I doubt we can make it tomorrow; Justin is away at the moment, you see.'

'I didn't realise,' Sonia said slowly.

'It's just a business trip,' she dismissed lightly. 'But we'll make arrangements for coming over to dinner as soon as he gets back,' she promised, willing her sister to leave now that she had said what she came here to say. Much more of Sonia's sympathetic looks and she would be crying all over her sister's silky dress!

'If you're going to be on your own this evening, why don't you come to us, anyway?' Sonia suggested eagerly. 'I'm sure it can't be any fun eating alone.'

She could just guess what interpretation Justin would put on her going to Sonia and Tony's for dinner! 'I'm really not sure when Justin is going to get back, and I'd like to be here when he does,' she refused with an apologetic smile.

'OK.' Sonia stood up to leave. 'But remember, you owe me.' Her eyes twinkled mischievously.

Caroline gave a start of surprise. 'I do?'

Sonia grinned, a perfectly natural smile that was nothing like the poses she affected in front of a camera. 'Paula hasn't exactly welcomed me as a member of the family, as my sister stole Justin right from under her nose. At least, I think it was her nose,' she added derisively.

Caroline couldn't help smiling at her sister's mischievous humour. 'She'll get over it,' she predicted with a relaxed smile, walking out with her sister to the door.

Sonia arched dark blonde brows. 'I don't know too many women that would "get over" a man like Justin!'

Caroline's smile remained fixed on her lips as she said goodbye to her sister, but her cheeks actually hurt from the strain of it by the time she returned to the lounge alone. Sonia was right; not many women would get over wanting someone like Justin. *She* would certainly never stop loving him!

She was in her room showering before dinner when she heard the apartment door opened, followed by Mrs Avery's surprised greeting, her pleasure obvious.

Justin. He had come home after all.

Her hands shook as she fastened the belt of her robe about her slim waist, putting up a self-conscious hand to her damp hair, its thick vibrancy drying in disordered waves. She had been going to blow-dry it into style as she usually did, but right now talking to Justin was of paramount importance. What did it matter that he would see her hair in its naturally wayward state for the first time? She doubted he would be much interested in her appearance anyway.

She faced him with wide eyes as the bedroom door opened seconds later and he stepped inside. He was dressed as he usually was for a day at work, his charcoal-grey suit perfectly tailored, his shirt pristine white, a silver-grey tie knotted at his throat. Had he been at work today after all?

'Caroline.' He nodded abruptly, putting his

briefcase down beside the bedroom chair, straightening his cuff as he turned to face her. 'Why do you look so pensive?' he regarded her coldly. 'Do you imagine I've returned home to beat you?'

She swallowed hard, hating it when he took on the guise of the successful lawyer he was. The man she loved was the fiercely gentle, always considerate lover that she had known in her bed every night since they had married—except for the last two nights.

She breathed raggedly. 'Have you?'

His mouth twisted as he loosened his tie, throwing off his jacket to place it over the back of the chair, an unusual thing for this usually fastidiously tidy man to do. 'Do I have reason to?' He arched dark brows.

'No,' she answered him unhesitantly.

He sat down in the chair, leaning back against his jacket, his eyes closed, seeming to forget her existence for the moment.

Caroline took the opportunity to look at him, to really look at him. He looked strained, lines of tiredness beside his eyes, his face paler than it usually was. In that moment he looked all of his thirty-six years, and Caroline longed to go to him, to kneel at his feet as she soothed the tension from his face. But there had been too much bitterness between them the last few days for her to be sure of her welcome, and she would break down completely if he rejected her.

Finally he roused himself, one hand moving to

the back of his nape to ease the pressure there, his gaze dark and disturbed as he looked at her across the width of the room.

Caroline was able to see the pain in his gaze then, the deep and utter despair that was so unlike the confident man she was used to.

'No,' he confirmed grimly.

She gave a puzzled frown, looking at him searchingly. 'No what?' she finally prompted in a voice husky with emotion.

He sighed. 'No, I have no reason to beat you.'

She didn't understand, puzzlement grooving a frown between her eyes. 'You aren't—angry, about the baby any more?' she questioned hesitantly.

He stood up so suddenly that she took a step backwards, receiving a mocking grimace at the involuntary movement. 'What's the use of being angry about the baby?' he dismissed harshly. 'It's a fact, isn't it?'

Her head went back in challenge. 'Yes.'

He nodded. 'That's what I thought,' he drawled uninterestedly. 'You—what have you done to your hair?' he frowned suddenly.

She put up a hand to the unruly swathe. 'I haven't had time to—to style it yet. Justin——'

'I like it.' He watched her, completely still, although restless energy permeated from him. 'It makes you look like a——Hell!' He swore viciously to himself. 'It's because I want you every damned time I look at you that we're in this mess in the first place, and as soon as I get home all I can think about is lying you back on that bed and feeling you

shudder against me!' He shook his head disgustedly, striding to the door to wrench it open.
'Get some clothes on,' he instructed coldly. 'I'll be
waiting in the lounge for you so that we can finish
this conversation.'

Caroline couldn't move for long minutes after he
had left, a small bud of hope pushing itself steadily
forward. Did his words mean that he accepted the
baby as his after all?

God, it was only a slight hope, but it galvanised
her into action. Quickly pulling clothes from the
cupboard to dress, the fawn loose-knit top she
wore a perfect colour match for her tailored
trousers, she left her hair as it was, not wanting to
waste the time on it just now.

Justin stood at the lounge window looking out
over London, dropping the curtain back in place to
turn and face her as he heard her entrance. He had
his thoughts and emotions completely back under
control now, his expression one of aloofness.

Caroline could only sigh for the passing of his
earlier lapse, knowing she couldn't hope to do
more than maintain her dignity when Justin
became this cold stranger.

She regarded him warily. 'Where were you last
night?'

He shrugged. 'At a hotel,' he dismissed curtly.
'It wouldn't have been a good idea for me to come
back here then,' he explained heavily.

Her lids lowered to hide the tears that suddenly
blurred her vision. 'At least you have come back,'
she said shakily.

'Yes,' he acknowledged derisively, 'but then this happens to be my apartment,' he reminded drily.

She looked at him accusingly. 'Our apartment,' she corrected firmly. 'If you're asking me to leave I would advise you to do it in a less subtle way than that,' she added in a hard voice. 'Because whether you believe it or not the child I'm carrying is yours. And I'll be damned——'

'I know,' he said quietly.

'—if I'll let you just——' Her voice trailed off weakly, and she stared at Justin with widely disbelieving eyes. She swallowed hard, so tense she felt as if she might snap in half. 'Did you just say—did you——'

'The child inside you is mine,' he confirmed flatly, his expression grim. 'Yesterday I returned to my doctor so that he could carry out tests to see if it were possible. Today,' he bit out harshly. 'he told me that the operation I had several years ago had somehow reversed itself, that I'm more than capable of fathering a child.' His mouth was tight with anger, boding ill for the doctor that had imparted this news to him.

Caroline's joyous relief at Justin's admission to being the father of her baby was quickly superseded by what he had said after that. She shook her head uncomprehendingly. 'I—operation?' she repeated dazedly. 'You don't mean a—a——'

'A vasectomy,' he supplied coldly, nodding abruptly. 'That's exactly what I do mean, Caroline,' he said impatiently.

Stunned disbelief was too mild a description of her emotions at that moment; she felt as if the breath had been completely knocked from her body, as if someone had dealt her a severely debilitating blow. Coloured spots of light danced before her eyes, and for a moment she felt as if she might faint.

'But—but *why?*' she cried when she at last found the strength to speak.

'Surely that's obvious?' Justin drawled.

'Not to me!' she groaned, her arms cradled about her stomach where their child nestled so innocently.

He gave an impatient sigh. 'I've already told you, I don't want children. The operation was supposed to ensure that I never had any,' he added with grating anger.

But what of the child she now carried?

CHAPTER FOUR

JUSTIN'S mouth twisted as he seemed to read the horrified question in her eyes. 'Yes,' he drawled, 'your pregnancy does seem to be rather a problem, doesn't it?'

The numbness fell away to be replaced by searing pain; Caroline knew without needing to be told that Justin still rejected their child. He was an aloof man, yes, often arrogant, but he could be kind, and he was always completely unselfish when they made love; what had made him dislike children so much that he had taken the drastic step of a vasectomy to ensure that he never had any? She knew that his own childhood had been happy, that he still deeply missed his mother who had died four years ago and his father who had followed her six months later, so it couldn't possibly be for that reason that he had decided never to have a family of his own.

She looked at him as if seeing him for the first time; she had never before known a person who simply disliked children, especially to the extreme Justin had gone to to avoid having any of his own.

He returned her gaze steadily for several seconds, and then pain clouded his gaze and he turned away. In that moment he looked completely vulnerable, as if a wound had opened up inside him and he didn't known how to stop the bleeding.

There was more, so much more to his decision not to have children than he was prepared to tell her, and she wanted so badly to know what it was, to be able to help him. But already his expression had become closed, as if he regretted even that tiny lapse in his guard.

'You want to have the baby, of course,' he bit out uninterestedly.

She stiffened. 'Of course.'

He nodded, as if he had never doubted what her answer would be. 'Then it would seem——'

'Justin, I don't want a divorce,' she cried, crossing the room to look up at him pleadingly. 'We don't talk about our feelings for each other, just seem to accept what we have——' her voice broke emotionally '—but I love you, Justin,' she told him raggedly. 'And I love your child that I carry inside me. Don't ask me to choose between the two of you!' She clasped his hands in entreaty, her eyes awash with tears.

He made no effort to return the clasp of her hands, but the didn't pull away from her either, his gaze dark as he looked down at her. 'I wouldn't do that,' he finally answered her gruffly. 'I don't think any woman's love should ever be tested to the extreme where she has to choose between her husband or her child. Besides,' he added self-derisively, 'I know I would lose.'

Her eyes clouded blue-grey. He was right; she would do anything he asked of her—except give up her child. Her hands dropped away from his, her cheeks ashen as she turned away. 'Do you want me to leave now, or—or will the morning do?'

'I don't want you to go at all.'

She spun around to face him, frowning heavily. And then she sighed. Of course he didn't want her to go, but they both knew she had to.

Her mouth twisted sadly. 'I hope I haven't disrupted your life too much the last few weeks. I tried not to——'

'Caroline, I said I don't want you to go,' he pointed out harshly.

'Yes, but——' She shook her head dazedly at his determined expression. 'What about the baby?' she reminded him softly, frowning.

He drew in a ragged breath. 'Isn't there room in your life for both of us?'

'Of course.' She shook her head in puzzlement. 'But you said——'

'And I meant it,' he cut in harshly. 'The child is yours, Caroline, and you must make what arrangements are needed for it. As long as it doesn't disrupt or disorganise my life, things can stay as they are,' he announced arrogantly.

Caroline gave an inward groan; babies were notorious for disrupting even the best laid plans, and they had a habit of disorganising on sight.

'We'll get a house outside London,' Justin continued distantly. 'That way the baby will be able to have its section of our living accommodation and I'll be able to have mine.'

And never the twain shall meet, thought

Caroline with a frown. What was *she* supposed to do. Distribute her attention between the two? She knew that was the general idea. Justin could have no idea of the amount of time that needed to be spent on a new baby, on a toddler, an infant; according to her mother the worrying and caring never stopped, even when the 'child' was as old as she was!

How could she agree to Justin's outline of the rest of their lives with any idea of being able to keep to it? What would it do to the child to grow up knowing its father was in the house but wanted nothing to do with it? But there was plenty of time before it would come to that, and in the meantime she might be able to persuade Justin into loving his child. From the coldness of his expression now that didn't look like much of a possibility, but it was all she had to hope for, loving him as much as she did.

'What if it doesn't work out?' she hesitated.

He sighed his impatience. 'I've made my compromise, Caroline, I can't offer any more.'

It was so much more than she had expected, but she knew the way he imagined them living would never work out, that children couldn't live by those rules. Maybe by the time Justin had realised that, he would have come to love his child after all. What choice did any of them have, unless she asked for the divorce without even trying to make her marriage work. That wasn't even a possible consideration. Once Justin had a child of his own, a son who looked like him, he might change his mind about not wanting children.

'I'll take it!' She gave a self-conscious grimace at his mockingly raised brows. 'I'm sorry, I didn't mean to make our marriage sound like a bargain I've just made.'

'We both know that a bargain is definitely something I'm not,' he derided. 'Now that that's settled I think I'll go to our bedroom and try to catch up on some of the sleep I missed the last two nights.' He looked at her warily. 'Caro?'

A blush of anticipation darkened her cheeks. 'I thought you said you wanted to catch up on your sleep?' she teased.

'I can do that later.' His gaze was intent. 'At the moment I need to make love to you. I don't want dinner,' he told her firmly as he guessed her intent to remind him they hadn't eaten yet. 'The sleep can wait. But I need *you* very much.'

That need was as close as he ever came to feeling anything for her, and with a man like Justin, a man who regarded most emotions as a weakness, it was the most she could expect for the moment.

'I need you, too,' she admitted softly. 'Justin——'

'Let's take one day at a time, Caro,' he advised gently. 'Starting with tonight.'

Their two nights apart had made them more eager for each other than ever, clothes landing where they were thrown, the two of them merging together without delay as they reacquainted themselves with each other's bodies. For Caroline, moments joined with Justin like this were the happiest in her life, a time when she felt truly one with him, when nothing could ever separate them.

Her own pinnacle reached, she loved nothing better than watching Justin as he lost all control, moving fiercely against him to increase his pleasure, loving the near-agony on his face as he shuddered into her in wave after wave of ecstasy. Tonight she joined him in this burning pleasure, knowing they had reached the ultimate in lovemaking.

'That was—that was——' Justin rested his damp forehead against hers, still moving spasmodically in lingering pleasure. 'I didn't hurt you?' He voiced his concern, knowing their lovemaking had been wilder tonight than ever before.

Caroline knew this would be his only acknowledgement of the baby she carried, that even though he didn't want it he wouldn't deliberately harm it. It was a start.

She caressed the sleek dampness of his back. 'Pain doesn't feel good,' she murmured throatily, 'and that felt very good!'

He chuckled softly, rolling to the bed at her side, taking her with him as he rested her head against his shoulder. 'I certainly didn't marry a shy virgin,' he said with satisfaction.

She had felt shy with him in the past, disturbed by his physical pull on her, but tonight she was filled with a new self-confidence.

'I like your hair like this.' He nuzzled against the wavy tresses. 'It makes you look like a wanton.' He laughed huskily as she buried her face against his chest. 'Not quite so wanton after all,' he murmured indulgently.

They lay quietly together, each savouring the aftermath of their passion, the new closeness that seemed to have sprung up from what Caroline had believed would be the end of them.

Suddenly Justin rolled over on to his stomach, his long fingers entangled in the softness of her hair as he gazed down at her intently. 'I still want you more than I have any other woman,' he told her intently.

Caroline smoothed the hair from his forehead, running a caressing finger over the black velvet eyepatch. 'I don't think I need to be assured of that at this moment,' she murmured indulgently, loving his weight on her.

'No,' he acknowledged heavily. 'But you said you love me, and I——I don't want to lose that love.'

Even though he couldn't love her in return. It was the first acknowledgement he had made of her admission earlier, and although her outburst had seemed to mean little to him at the time she could now see that it mattered to him very much, that he deeply regretted not being able to feel the same emotion for her. But she had gone into this marriage with her eyes wide open, and besides, she knew that he did feel something for her, otherwise he would have ended the marriage as soon as he found out about the baby. Instead he had chosen to find a compromise, one that was going to be difficult to live up to, certainly, but he had been determined to keep her in his life, as his wife.

'Has knowing I don't want our child made you hate me?' he ground out intently.

Her expression softened, but Justin wasn't looking at her; his gaze unseeing, he was lost inside himself.

'Children are such vulnerable creatures, you see,' he murmured raggedly. 'The most vulnerable things in the world . . .' He trembled against her. 'I can't love our child, Caroline; I'm sorry.' He lay his head against her breast, just like the vulnerable child he was so afraid of caring about.

Caroline continued to hold him, feeling very protective at that moment. Justin was afraid of love, and loving; she would just have to surround him with so much of it he couldn't escape feeling the emotion himself. She could do it, could do anything now that she knew he cared for her enough not to let anything end their marriage.

A lot of women in Caroline's situation would have felt miserable over the sudden change that had come over their life, but all mixed up with Justin's aversion to their child was his new-found tenderness with her. In some strange, elusive way, they were closer than they had ever been.

They never talked about the baby, and yet Caroline knew they were both very aware of its existence, that it made Justin softer and more approachable.

For three days they lived in a romantic glow, Caroline filled with an inner peace that had her running to greet Justin when he arrived home from

work in the evenings, both of them eager for the
time they could close the bedroom door behind
them and just forget everything but each other.

It couldn't last, of course, and the intrusion
came in the form of a telephone call from her
sister.

'Well?' Sonia demanded without preamble.
'You can't tell me Justin is still away on business!'

The invitation for dinner! She had forgotten all
about it in the tension of Justin's return and his
subsequent decision to carry on with their marriage
and ignore the fact that she carried his child.

'Er—no——'

'Then why haven't you called?' Sonia reproved
impatiently. 'I know it isn't going to be the most
pleasant of evenings,' she conceded with a sigh,
'but for the sake of the family we can't go on
avoiding it.'

When Simon had called around briefly yesterday
evening he had seemed to find the whole situation
rather funny. Sonia's twin in every way, he
couldn't bring himself to be serious about anything
for more than two minutes, and the predicament of
his two sisters, with Sonia marrying Caroline's ex-
boyfriend, really seemed to amuse him. Having
been the brunt of his practical jokes most of her
life, and having taken them all in good humour,
Caroline couldn't feel angry with him over
something that had been of Sonia's and her own
making. Justin seemed to consider her young
brother needed a year's hard labour to make him
see the serious side of life!

'No,' she accepted softly. 'OK, I'll talk to Justin about it tonight.' She grimaced at the thought of bringing this note of disharmony into their new rapport.

'You mean you haven't even spoken to him about it yet?' Sonia groaned.

'You and Tony haven't been our main topic of conversation recently, no,' she answered impatiently.

'That's a pity,' Sonia drawled drily. 'You and Justin have been ours.'

'Why?' she asked bluntly.

'Tony said he's seen you around the hospital a couple of times recently and you seem very distracted.'

She smiled. 'So you and he have been speculating as to whether or not the honeymoon is over?' she derided without rancour.

'Well . . . not exactly.' Sonia's squirm of discomfort could be heard in her voice. 'But we have been concerned about you, yes.'

'Well you needn't be,' she dismissed briskly. 'Justin and I are very happy together,' she said with a confidence she had only known the last three days. 'However, I do have something I want to talk to you about when we come over,' she added enigmatically, deliberately obscure, knowing the enjoyment of teasing her sister as she imagined Sonia's impatience to know what she wanted to talk about.

As a child, Sonia had always found it impossible to keep a secret, either her own or anyone else's, and she hadn't changed over the years, always hating having to wait for anything.

'Tell me now,' she predictably encouraged, her eagerness evident in her voice.

'I'd rather not,' Caroline dismissed lightly, mischief shining in her eyes as she smiled to herself. She was going to see her parents after work that evening to tell them about the baby; dinner with Sonia and Tony would be the ideal time to tell them about it, too. 'It's rather—personal,' she added confidingly, still smiling teasingly.

'Do you want me to call round tonight?' her sister instantly offered. 'It wouldn't be much out of my way, and if it's so urgent——'

'Oh, it isn't urgent,' Caroline assured her softly. 'It can wait until Justin and I come over for dinner.'

Although she doubted her sister could, she acknowledged indulgently as she rang off. Christmas had always been an exhausting affair with Sonia around, her young sister refusing to let anyone go back to sleep on Christmas morning after she had woken up, demanding that she see everyone else's presents besides her own. Waiting until Caroline went over for dinner before knowing what she wanted to talk about was going to be a severe strain on her.

Her parents, as she had known they would be, were ecstatic at the thought of becoming grandparents, and as she listened to them chattering about the exciting event she was glad to be able to give them something back, besides her love, for all that they had given her.

An older version of Sonia, tall and blonde and beautiful, her mother, at almost fifty, still retained the elegant slenderness that her younger daughter had also inherited. The love between her and her tall and handsome husband was a tangible thing. That love had surrounded Caroline, Sonia and Simon when they, too, had lived at home, but like all parents theirs had realised when it was time to let go so that their children could seek out loves of their own. Caroline knew that they found Justin a little aloof, that they were even a little in awe of him, but they did approve of him, of the happiness he had given their eldest daughter. And they were overjoyed at the thought of the baby.

Her smile turned to a niggling frown during the drive home as she wondered how best to approach Justin with the idea of dinner with Sonia and Tony. She knew without being told that he wouldn't be thrilled at the idea; he hadn't forgotten yet that she had been involved with Tony when the two of them had met, his bitter accusations when she first told him about the baby proof of that. But they couldn't go on avoiding her sister and her husband for the rest of their lives, not unless they wanted to continue making things unpleasant for all her family. Except Simon, of course, who would no doubt carry on finding it amusing.

Mrs Avery had left for the evening, the dinner almost ready, when Caroline heard her husband's key in the lock. She tensed as if for a fight. Damn, and things had been going so well for them lately!

'Mmm.' Justin drew back slightly after accepting her kiss hello, his linked hands at the curve of her spine bringing them into intimate contact. 'How long can dinner wait?' he urged with husky intent.

'It can't,' she said regretfully.

'Pity,' he drawled as he went to their bedroom to freshen up, his arm about her waist as she accompanied him.

Perhaps it was a little early in their marriage for Justin's desire for her to have waned, but even so, his way of always making her feel desirable filled her with a warm glow.

She watched with unashamed enjoyment as he undressed before stepping under the shower, loving the lean beauty of his body, an excited heat coming to her cheeks. She was waiting outside the shower cubicle with a towel for him to drape about his hips when he stepped out from under the hot spray, and she sat on the side of the bath as she watched him take his second shave of the day, a dark shadow left on his jaw even after this was accomplished.

Their gazes met often in the mirror as Justin drew the blade smoothly over his chin, a fire kindling there, becoming a flame, finally raging into burning desire, hungry for each other as Justin finally turned to sweep her up in his arms and carry her through to the bedroom.

'I don't care what's going to spoil for dinner,' he muttered as he threw off her clothes with practised ease. 'You can't look at me like that and then expect me to meekly sit down and eat dinner!' he growled in a voice that spoke of his arousal.

This man had never been meek about anything, and she revelled in his fierce lovemaking, matching his passion as she was the one to take them both into that swirling vortex where she could only cling to Justin as her stability to stop her floating away completely.

They dressed slowly and leisurely, sharing intimate smiles, laughing softly together as they served up the dried chicken and overcooked vegetables; Caroline was sure that neither of them noticed what they were eating anyway as they ate without taking their gazes off each other.

'Will you—will you ever show me under that?' Caroline looked pointedly at the eye-patch. 'It doesn't matter if you'd rather not,' she rushed into speech as she realised what she had done. 'I realise it must be very painful for you to look at and—oh!' She stared at him transfixed as he moved one slender hand up and brought the black velvet patch up on to his forehead.

A scar ran from just below his eyebrow to his upper cheek, a thin silver line that looked deceptively harmless, the real damage the blade had done as it sliced through his flesh obvious as he looked at her with his sightless eye, the iris so light a grey it seemed almost colourless, the pupil that same void.

It wasn't an ugly scar to look upon; it was the thought of the wound that caused the cold shiver down her spine. She knew every inch of Justin's body intimately, knew that he had no other scars but this one, which implied that the damage that man *had* done he had done deliberately. To deliberately try to blind Justin——! The thought made her feel ill.

Justin settled the patch back into place, calmly pouring more wine for both of them, watching with satisfaction as Caroline took a swallow of hers. 'Did you go and see your parents this evening?' he asked conversationally—just as if he hadn't, in effect, bared his pain to her.

'Yes,' she confirmed dismissively, her hand covering his as it rested on the table top. 'Justin, I'm not repulsed by your scar,' she told him earnestly. 'I'm just—sickened by the thought of what you suffered!' Her voice told him of the pain she now suffered with him.

He shrugged. 'It happened some time ago now. You've seen it, now let's just forget it,' he advised harshly.

She should never have asked this of him tonight, should have realised, when they were both trying so hard to make their marriage work, that he wouldn't be able to say no!

'I'm sorry, Justin.' She squeezed his hand. 'I shouldn't have pried.'

His gaze was very tense. 'Some things are better left as they are,' he agreed in a hard voice. 'Do you want a piece of burnt apple pie?' His mood softened slightly as they both recalled the reason the food had been over-cooked. 'Or shall we go through to the living-room and have coffee?' He quirked dark brows.

She nodded, standing up. 'At least that won't be burnt!'

Justin was glancing through some papers from his briefcase when she entered the room with the coffee things, putting them away as soon as he heard her approach, although it would take a little longer for him to put his role as lawyer away, she knew from experience. It could be a little unnerving living with a man who could be both harsh stranger and tender lover, but she was learning to cope with it.

'Mum and Dad send their love,' she began to chatter as she poured their coffee. 'Dad is in the middle of some business deal at the moment, and Mum is coping with seeing him through it, as usual. Dad makes the worst salesman I ever knew.' She smiled indulgently, relieved to see the tension was leaving Justin as she continued to chatter her nonsense. 'But somehow he seems to be successful at it.' At forty-five her father had been forced to make a career change, and for the last five years he had been involved in the sale of computers. He was an easy, charming man, able to put most people at their ease, and yet he seemed to go to pieces every time he made a large sale. It was a cause of great teasing from his family.

'He has charisma,' Justin said drily.

'Yes.' She sobered, looking across at him uncertainly. 'I told them about the baby.'

He nodded; not by so much as a flick of an eyelid did he show that the subject disturbed or displeased him. 'I thought that you might,' he acknowledged distantly.

'They're thrilled for us,' she added awkwardly.

He gave an inclination of his head. 'I expected that, too.'

She felt a stab of pain at his lack of interest, and then berated herself; it was too soon for him to feel anything else. They had months yet before the baby was born.

She looked at him beneath lowered lashes, unable to gauge his reaction to her next announcement. 'Sonia telephoned me at work today.' She waited breathlessly for him to say something, anything; when he didn't, just raised questioning brows, she rushed into speech again. 'She and Tony have invited us over for dinner.'

Once again he showed no emotion. 'Did you accept?' he said curiously.

A blush darkened her cheeks. 'I wouldn't do that without talking to you first.' She shook her head.

'And is that what you were doing earlier—talking to me?' His voice was harsh.

Her eyes widened at his implication that their love-making had been in the form of a bribe on her part.

His mouth twisted at her pained incredulity. 'Isn't that the way all wives get around their husbands?' he derided. 'Give him a little of what he wants and then you can take a whole lot of what you want?'

She was hurt that he could think she would be that devious, very much so, and her first instinct was to tell him to go to hell. But they had come such a long way the last three days; she didn't want to lose that because of a cynical misunderstanding on Justin's part.

'I didn't say that I particularly *want* to go to dinner with Sonia and Tony,' she returned, her eyes steady on his.

His gaze narrowed. 'Why not?'

'But then again I didn't say that I *didn't* want to go either,' she said lightly. 'I'm going to leave that decision completely up to you.'

'Damned if I do and damned if I don't?' he drawled ruefully, his mood softening slightly.

Caroline smiled. 'Not really. It's going to be awkward for all of us, and if you would rather not——'

'We'll go,' he decided with his usual arrogance. 'It's time the awkwardness was brought to an end,' he added determinedly.

She nodded. 'I'll call Sonia tomorrow and tell her. In the meantime,' her eyes glowed with mischief, 'could I offer you another—bribe?'

Justin gave a groan of self-disgust as he stood up and crossed the room to her side, coming down on his haunches, touching her cheek gently. 'That was a hell of a thing for me to have said,' he admitted with a sigh. 'I'm sorry, Caroline.'

She met the intensity of his gaze, smoothing back the dark swathe of his hair. 'Not Caro?' she encouraged in a husky voice.

'*Always* Caro,' he admitted ruefully. 'Let's leave all this for Mrs Avery to clear away in the morning and go to bed, hm?' he encouraged softly.

She shook her head, laughing huskily as Justin frowned his disappointment. 'I meant I'll get up early in the morning and clear these things away,' she mocked, standing up. *'Not* that I didn't think it was a good idea to go to bed. You know what they say about pregnant woman——' She broke off, looking up at him with stricken eyes.

'No,' he returned smoothly, his arm about her waist as they walked to their bedroom. 'What do they say?'

Caroline's breath left her in a relieved sigh. She had been so afraid . . . But it seemed the subject of her pregnancy wasn't a taboo one; only Justin's enthusiasm for it. Well, she had never thought these next months were going to be easy!

She stood up on tiptoe and whispered in his ear exactly what was said about the hormones of pregnant women.

His gaze widened teasingly as he straightened, humour glinting in the depths of silver-grey. 'You mean you're going to get even *more* demanding?' he sighed. 'Try and remember I'm an old man, Caroline.'

She smiled at his reminder of what she had told him the night they met. 'Older men make the best lovers,' she said pertly—and then held her breath as she realised she had once again said the wrong thing after Justin's recent suspicions that Tony had been her lover.

His expression softened as he saw her self-reproach. 'How would you know?' he teased softly. 'You've only ever had one lover!'

She needed no other assurance that he believed her about that now.

But that wasn't going to make having dinner with Sonia and Tony any easier; she wasn't looking forward to it at all.

CHAPTER FIVE

TO ALL intents and purposes they were just two couples about to spend the evening together, but beneath the surface politeness of their initial greetings Tony's mood was slightly morose, and Justin watched them all with a speculative gaze.

Sonia had lost no time in making the arrangements for that very evening once Caroline had telephoned her and told her she and Justin accepted her invitation. Maybe she had thought they might try to get out of it if she allowed any time to elapse. Whatever the reason for her haste, they were all together now, and it was left to Caroline and Sonia to keep the conversation going, chatting about general things while the two men eyed each other in male challenge.

Sonia was looking her usual beautiful self, and the apartment they had bought and that she had decorated reflected her sunny personality, the bright oranges and lemons in the lounge only slightly subdued by small touches of brown. Tony seemed very well, as if married life suited him, too, although his dark frown ruined his charming good looks slightly; he obviously still hadn't quite forgiven Caroline for marrying Justin, despite the fact that he had found happiness with her sister!

'Having you back certainly seems to suit Caroline,' Sonia told Justin mischievously. 'She looked quite wan while you were away on business.'

'I seem to remember your telling me I looked beautiful that day,' Caroline reminded drily.

'Well, you did, darling,' her sister nodded. 'You always do. But you looked a little lost, too.'

She cast Justin an uncomfortable look, knowing by the teasing glitter in his gaze that he found her sister's chatter amusing.

'I wasn't lost at all,' she told Sonia impatiently, avoiding Tony's somewhat scornful gaze. 'I had plenty to keep me busy. And you came to call. And so did——Oh!' She gave a stricken groan as she realised she had forgotten to tell Justin about the visit from his friend, Don Lindford. 'Oh dear! Justin, I'm so sorry.' She gave a rueful grimace. 'With all that was happening I just forgot, and——'

'Darling, what are you talking about?' he prompted with indulgent humour.

'You had a visitor while you were away, and I completely forgot to tell you.' She shook her head in self-disgust. 'And Mr Lindford seemed so nice, too——'

'Mr who?' Justin prompted quietly, sitting forward in his chair.

'Don Lindford,' she explained awkwardly. 'I really am sorry I forgot to tell you. But he did say he would be in touch again soon, and that—that he was sorry to have missed you,' she ended lamely.

She knew very well why she had forgotten to tell Justin that the other man had called: Sonia's visit coming shortly afterwards, and then Justin's own traumatic return. Under the circumstances it wasn't really surprising she had forgotten Don Lindford's visit, but even so it was a little shameful when he was the first and only friend of Justin's she had ever met!

'I *am* sorry,' she said again, grimacing.

Justin seemed lost in thought, his expression harsh. She knew it had been thoughtless of her to omit telling him about the other man, but he really didn't need to look so angry about it; Don had said he would come back!

'Did he stay long?' Justin finally bit out into the uncomfortable silence, Sonia looking puzzled by the exchange, Tony regarding them with narrow-eyed speculation.

Caroline's cheeks burnt as she hurriedly looked away from Tony's mocking expression. He seemed to be saying, 'Are you still sure you married the right man?'

'Only a few minutes,' she answered Justin. 'He didn't seem to have a lot of time. I offered him a cup of tea, but he refused, and——'

'What did he talk about?' Justin prompted harshly.

'Nothing, really.' She shook her head dismissively. 'I told you, he didn't have a lot of time. Was his visit important?' She looked at him frowningly.

For a moment it didn't seem that he would

answer, and then he drew in a ragged breath, shaking off his stormy mood with effort. 'No, I don't suppose so,' he grated. 'I'll try and get in touch with him myself, although he can be a little elusive. But if he calls around again perhaps you could let me know immediately?' He arched dark brows.

He was displeased with her omission, that was completely obvious, and the last thing she had wanted was to show any sign of dissension between the two of them in front of Sonia and Tony. She took the only way she could to cover up the strain she now felt under.

'Justin and I have some wonderful news,' she smiled brightly, ignoring his frowning look. 'I'm going to have a baby!' she announced at their questioning looks.

'How lovely!' Sonia cried enthusiastically, missing her husband's sudden loss of humour as she threw her arms about Caroline and hugged her.

'When's it due?'

Caroline turned sharply to Tony as he addressed her directly for the first time this evening, aware of Sonia's sudden tension as she still stood with her arms about her. Things were obviously still far from perfect between her sister and Tony!

Her head went back challengingly as she met Tony's mocking gaze. 'In just over seven months' time.' Her expression dared him to dispute that.

'A honeymoon baby; how wonderful!' Sonia recovered quickly, smiling at Caroline with genuine pleasure.

'Not exactly,' Justin drawled. 'Caroline and I never actually had a honeymoon.' He looked at her. 'Maybe now would be a good time for it,' he murmured softly.

She blushed at the warm desire in his gaze, feeling hot all over at the thought of several weeks alone with Justin, with nothing to do but please each other. It sounded like heaven!

'Champagne!' Sonia announced excitedly. 'We have to have champagne to celebrate. Tony, pop down to the off-licence and——'

'It really isn't necessary,' Caroline put in hastily before he could come back with some cutting retort, knowing that, in the mood he was in tonight, he was more than capable of it. 'I probably shouldn't be drinking alcohol in my condition, anyway,' she dismissed lightly.

'One glass of champagne isn't going to hurt you—or the baby,' Sonia insisted. 'Tony?' she prompted again, her voice firm.

Caroline held her breath, knowing that Justin wouldn't stand for it if the other man said anything insulting.

'Why not?' Tony drawled, getting slowly to his feet, very handsome in black fitted trousers and an open-necked green shirt. 'Why don't you come with me, Justin?' he suggested as he pulled on his jacket. 'I'm sure the women would welcome the chance for one of those girl-to-girl chats they seem so fond of!' He looked questioningly at the other man. 'Especially as they have something so interesting to chat about,' he added tauntingly.

Justin stood up, coldly meeting the other man's gaze. 'A short walk while the women finish preparing dinner sounds like a good idea,' he nodded.

Tony gave him a scornful look as the two of them walked to the door. 'We'll be lucky if we get any dinner at all tonight after Caroline's announcement! After you.' He held the door open with a flourish.

'Don't wives, especially pregnant ones, get a kiss goodbye any more?' Sonia teased them both.

Tony walked towards her. 'There isn't anything you're not telling me, is there?' He kissed her briefly on the lips.

'Believe me, the day I find out I'm carrying your child I'll be shouting it from the rooftops,' Sonia assured him huskily.

Caroline turned away from the intimacy of the moment, grimacing a little as Justin frowned down at her, obviously unhappy with being put in this position, a man who could only show his affection in private. And she knew he was still a little angry with her about Don Lindford.

She moved up to kiss him lightly on the mouth, frozen for an instant as he deepened the caress before moving abruptly away again, as if he regretted the impulse.

She stared after him a little dazedly as he left with Tony.

Sonia giggled at her side. 'It hasn't been half as bad as I'd imagined,' she admitted at Caroline's questioning look. 'I thought the two of them might resort to pistols at dawn, fisticuffs at least,' she reported happily. 'I think I'm a little disappointed that they've gone off together to buy champagne instead.' She wrinkled her nose prettily.

'Sonia!' Caroline reproved in a shocked voice; the last thing she needed was any more turbulence because of her marriage to Justin.

Her sister sat down, patting the sofa at her side for Caroline to do the same thing. 'Not that I would have wanted them to hurt each other or anything like that——' her eyes gleamed with mischief —'but I'd simply love to see your Justin without his usual control!'

Caroline couldn't help returning her smile as she settled down next to her on the sofa. 'Believe me, it doesn't happen very often.'

'Really?' Blonde brows rose over laughing blue eyes. 'And I would have said, just from looking at him, that he's a very sensual man!'

Caroline gave her a reproving look. 'That's for me to know—and no other woman ever to find out!' she added teasingly.

Sonia laughed softly. 'We don't need to; anyone looking at you can see you're very—satisfied, with your marriage.'

'Liberated as Mum and Dad are, I think they might be a little shocked at the way their "baby" is talking right now,' Caroline drawled.

Sonia sobered. 'I can't believe my big sister is going to have a baby of her own very soon.' She shook her head sadly. 'It doesn't seem that long since we were playing with our dolls!'

'No.' Caroline became lost in those happy memories, too.

'Is Justin pleased?'

She focused frowningly on her sister. 'Sorry?'

'Is Justin pleased about the baby?' Sonia repeated lightly. 'He didn't say a lot, so I wondered . . .' She looked at Caroline questioningly.

'Oh, you know,' she shrugged. 'Men are always a bit flattened by pregnancy,' she evaded.

'Hm,' Sonia nodded, her attention already wandering from Justin and his reaction to becoming a father. 'I wonder if that's what Tony and I need?'

Caroline's hand covered Sonia's restless one; she saw the bewilderment in her sister's eyes as she allowed her cheerful guard to slip for a brief moment. 'Don't have a child expecting it to hold the marriage together,' she advised gently. 'Often it does the opposite.'

Sonia shrugged off her despondency, her dazzling smile back in place. 'I don't need anything to keep Tony happy but little old me,' she grinned. 'Let's surprise them and have dinner ready when they get back.' She stood up to pull Caroline to her feet. 'Another few months and you'll need a crane to do that,' she announced cheerfully on her way to the kitchen she had decorated in blue and white; she had told Caroline when she showed her around on their arrival that, as it was the room she intended spending the least amount of time in, it could have more conservative colours.

'Thanks,' she said drily as they set about draining the vegetables and carving the meat.

They had barely placed the food on the table when the men arrived back, the two of them arguing good-naturedly about their taste in literature.

It was the fact that it was good-natured banter that surprised Caroline, who gave the two men puzzled glances as there no longer seemed that tension between them that had been all too evident earlier in the evening.

'A toast.' Tony stood up once the champagne had been poured. 'To Caroline and Justin—and the cub they're expecting,' he added teasingly.

Caroline barely had time to register his mocking humour before she became aware that Justin was standing up, his champagne quickly dampening his trousers, his glass on the floor.

Her first thought was had he done it on purpose, so that he didn't have to drink a toast to a child he didn't want and couldn't love? And then she knew he wouldn't be so petty, that it had to have been a genuine accident.

Only seconds had passed by the time she reached that conclusion, but it had been long enough for Sonia to have brought him a towel from the bathroom so that he could mop up the surface dampness.

'Never mind, old chap,' Tony mocked. 'I'd be a nervous wreck, too, if I were about to be a father.'

Justin handed the damp towel back to Sonia. 'I think we'll have to go, Caroline,' he announced regretfully, grimacing as he pulled the damp material away from his thighs.

'Borrow a pair of my trousers,' Tony offered as he

saw how disappointed Sonia looked. 'We're about the same size, and I won't mind if you won't.' He looked challengingly at the other man. 'It was probably my fault anyway,' he pulled a face. 'Alluding to the fact that everyone calls you The Wolf. Behind your back, of course,' he added drily.

Justin turned to an ashen-faced Caroline. 'Not always behind my back,' he murmured softly, rewarded with the delicate blush that tinged Caroline's cheeks. Since that first night, when she had learnt that he knew of the nickname after all, she had always cried out that name when they made love!

'I see,' Tony drawled suggestively. 'Well, let's not break up the evening just because of a little spilt champagne,' he dismissed.

Caroline stared down at her hands after the two men had gone into the bedroom. It had to have been an accident—didn't it?

'Don't look so upset,' Sonia cajoled gently. 'Personally I'm glad of a good excuse for the food being awful,' she confided with a grimace.

She couldn't help chuckling at her sister's self-derisive humour, and was still smiling when Tony rejoined them.

It was several minutes before Justin came out of the bedroom, too, and Caroline's eyes widened as she took in the grey pair of trousers that Tony had leant him. Much more modern than anything she had seen Justin in before, with their fitted waist and baggy style, they nonetheless made him look more rakishly attractive than ever.

'I should watch it, old man,' Tony drawled as he

looked at Caroline knowingly. 'I know that look from living with her sister; it means your wardrobe is about to undergo a complete change!'

Justin returned the smile, resuming his seat at the table. 'I don't think they would be very suitable for the courtroom,' he mocked.

'Oh, Caroline won't be sending you to work in them,' Tony informed him confidently. 'Some other woman might appreciate that more than she would like. No, she'll be more interested in getting you *out* of them when you're at home.'

'Tony!' his wife scolded as Caroline could only blush. 'Propose the toast again and keep your thoughts to yourself.'

'See what I mean,' he told the other man resignedly. 'It's wicked when you're just a sex-symbol.'

Caroline shared her laughter with Justin; when Tony was in this mood he was irresistible!

'Let me propose the toast,' Justin spoke softly, holding up his glass that Tony had refilled. 'To my beautiful wife.'

Her blush deepened at the obvious pride in his voice.

'Don't forget the baby,' Sonia reminded him impatiently.

He only hesitated for a fraction of a second, not enough for Sonia and Tony to see his reluctance, but too long for Caroline to be unaware of it. 'And the baby,' he added abruptly, sipping the bubbly wine.

Caroline needed more than a sip, but the bubbles tickled her nose and made her eyes water.

'I'm afraid the dinner is going to be ruined now,'

Sonia announced with an innocently regretful voice.

Caroline took one look at her sister, Sonia glanced back, and the two of them burst into laughter.

'It's all right, Justin,' Tony said drily when he saw him looking at them in surprise. 'If you had eaten your dinner while it was still hot you would have found that my wife had ruined the meal long ago. I usually advise people to bring along something for indigestion!'

'Tony Shepherd! How dare you!'

'Don't worry, she isn't really mad,' Tony assured them confidently. 'If she were really angry she would have called me "Anthony Graham Shepherd",' he said knowingly. 'She can't really be angry with me when she knows I'm telling the truth, you see.' He shrugged.

'Tony!' Sonia groaned in acute embarrassment. 'What's Justin going to think?'

'Before or after I've tried the food?' Justin drily joined in the teasing.

'Caroline, you never told me Justin can be cruel.' Sonia pretended to be hurt by their humour at her expense, although the laughter in her eyes belied the impression a little.

What she had expected to be a disaster of an evening, Caroline had found pleasantly enjoyable. The food wasn't half as bad as Sonia had claimed it would be; in fact it was rather nice, despite being a little cold. And the company was certainly scintillating. There had been a few awkward moments, but in the circumstances that was only to be expected; all in all it had been a successful evening.

Justin was very quiet on the drive home, and Caroline glanced at him searchingly several times.

'It went well, I thought.' Finally she couldn't stand the silence any longer.

He frowned. 'What? Oh—yes,' he nodded vaguely.

She grimaced, putting her hand on his thigh, instantly feeling him tense beneath her touch. 'Are you still angry with me?' she coaxed. 'Because I forgot to mention your friend's visit,' she explained at his puzzled expression.

Justin gave a heavy sigh. 'I'm not angry with you at all. I wish you had remembered to tell me sooner, but I'm certainly not angry with you.'

'Then why—never mind,' she dismissed with a strained smile. 'What did you say to Tony when the two of you went out for champagne?' she probed teasingly. 'He certainly seemed in a better mood when he got back.'

His mouth twisted. 'We didn't fight it out, if that's what you mean.

She sobered. 'No, of course that isn't what I meant,' she said impatiently. 'He just seemed— different, when the two of you got back.'

Justin shrugged. 'Maybe he realised he no longer has a chance with you. How would I know why he was different—if he was,' he muttered irritably.

Tony *had* been much more amenable after he and Justin went out for champagne, and even Justin had to have realised that. But if he didn't want to talk about that change, or the reason for it, she knew there was nothing she could do or say to make him

WOW!

THE MOST GENEROUS
FREE OFFER EVER!

From the Harlequin Reader Service

NO COST! NO OBLIGATION!
NO PURCHASE NECESSARY!

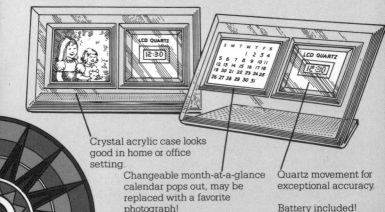

HARLEQUIN PRESENTS NOVELS
FREE!

Harlequin Reader Service®

```
AFFIX
FOUR FREE BOOKS
STICKER HERE
```

YES, send me my free books and gifts as explained
on the opposite page. I have affixed my "free books"
sticker above and my two "free gifts" stickers below.
I understand that accepting these books and gifts
places me under no obligation ever to buy any books;
I may cancel at any time, for any reason, and the free
books and gifts will be mine to keep!   108 CIH CANP

NAME
_____
                    (PLEASE PRINT)

ADDRESS _____ APT. _____

CITY _____

STATE _____ ZIP _____

```
AFFIX FREE
CLOCK/CALENDAR
STICKER HERE
```

```
AFFIX FREE
MYSTERY GIFT
STICKER HERE
```

WE EVEN PROVIDE FREE POSTAGE!

It costs you *nothing* to send for your free books — we've paid the postage on the attached reply card. And we'll pick up the postage on your shipment of free books and gifts, and also on any subsequent shipments of books, should you choose to become a subscriber. Unlike many book clubs, we charge *nothing* for postage and handling!

do so.

Justin's strangely taciturn mood persisted even once they had showered and prepared for bed, and for the first time since they were married Justin turned out his bedside lamp and lay with his back towards her.

She tentatively touched his bare shoulder. 'Justin?'

'Go to sleep, Caroline,' he told her harshly, his back still towards her.

'But——'

'I'm tired, Caroline.' He turned on her angrily, his gaze glittering in the darkness. 'We don't have to make love every night!' he added scornfully.

She drew her hand away as if she had been burnt, blinking back the tears, her throat aching as she tried to stop them flowing. 'I'm sorry,' she said in a choked voice. 'I didn't realise. I thought—it's just that this is the first time you haven't wanted me . . .' Her hurt was reflected in her eyes.

Justin looked angrier than ever. 'And after almost two months, isn't it due?' he attacked.

Her tongue ran along the dryness of her lips. 'I suppose so . . . I—of course.' She turned away blindly, lying in the darkness with her eyes wide open, finding it more and more difficult to hold back the tears.

If she had expected him to relent, to apologise for his bad humour, she was out of luck. The only movement he made in the bed was to settle down with his back towards her once again, and within minutes the deep evenness of his breathing told her that he had fallen asleep.

She at last allowed the tears to fall. Why had she assumed Justin would always want her? Maybe she was being unreasonable expecting him to make love to her every night; after all, he didn't have to want her all the time, and maybe he really was tired.

But he didn't have to be so cruel about it, could even have held her in his arms until they both fell asleep. He had wanted to hurt her for some reason.

Maybe he had changed his mind about accepting the baby because he wanted her so much. Maybe he no longer wanted her. But that didn't ring true, not after the way he had tried to persuade her into bed when she was all dressed and ready to go to Sonia's and Tony's for dinner! He had been eager enough then, teasing her when she almost forgot Sonia and Tony completely and gave in. As he had drawn away from her he had promised to make love to her later until she begged for mercy. Instead he had rejected her, turned his back on her, and then fallen asleep. It didn't make sense to her at all.

She glanced longingly at the golden smoothness of his back, hungering for contact with him, but fearful of rejection once again. Instead she lay on her back staring sightlessly up at the ceiling, sure that she wasn't going to be able to sleep.

She awoke to the realisation that something was wrong, very wrong.

It took her several seconds to shake off the disorientation of a deep sleep, to realise that it was still dark outside, that she could feel the warmth of Justin's body beside her own.

Then what had awoken her, because something surely had? Could it be that——

'No, damn it!' Justin suddenly ground out fiercely at her side, his tension a tangible thing. 'No!' he groaned again. 'You can't. I won't let you. Oh, dear God!'

Caroline had scrambled into a sitting position at his first outcry, moving to soothe his brow now, murmuring reassuringly to him as he seemed in the grips of a horrific nightmare.

'It's all right, Justin,' she crooned. 'It's all right darling. Justin——'

'Penny!' He gave an anguished shout.

Caroline recoiled as if he had struck her. Who on earth was Penny?

CHAPTER SIX

'SO IF you can think of somewhere you would like to go, I can arrange to be free all of next week.' Justin looked at her indulgently.

Somehow trying to think of where they could go on their belated honeymoon didn't hold all that much appeal for Caroline when she wasn't even sure they had a marriage any more.

It wasn't just that Justin hadn't made love to her for three days, and nights; it was that he was still having those dreams at night, and each time he did he called out for the woman called Penny. She still had no idea who the other woman was, but the love and anguish in Justin's voice when he spoke of her was obvious.

Love. Yes, the emotion Justin had warned her he could never feel for *her,* she knew he felt for the other woman.

Caroline's own anguish had begun the very first time he had cried the other woman's name, an emotional torment that didn't leave her day or night. If Justin loved this woman called Penny, why wasn't it her he had married? Unless, she had guessed, when no other explanation seemed to make sense, Penny was already married and so unnattainable to him? It made his decision to marry *her,* when he admitted to only feeling desire for her, rather more understandable.

The last thing she felt like doing now, however, was planning a honeymoon trip for herself and Justin. What was the point of a honeymoon when the two of them didn't even touch any more unless it was by accident? And she couldn't bear the idea of the two of them going off to be alone somewhere with Justin's thoughts of Penny being a very intrusive third.

God, she was glad he hadn't tried to make love to her the last three days; she wasn't sure she would have been able to respond even if he *had* touched her!

He hadn't told her he had had a vasectomy, and he had lied when he scorned love; he was definitely in love with this Penny. Maybe even his initial decision not to have children had something to do with the other woman, or perhaps that was the reason the two of *them* weren't married; it would be difficult for any woman to accept Justin's decision not to have children, and the steps he had taken to ensure it never happened.

Whatever the reason, Justin wasn't with the woman he loved but was married to her instead, and she didn't feel as if she could go on a honeymoon with him as if nothing had changed between them. Oh, her love for Justin would never change, she had known that when she had been able to accept his conditions concerning her having the baby, but it was no longer a love she felt able to give unreservedly.

'I'm really not worried about going anywhere, Justin,' she dismissed shruggingly. 'I would have to take time off from the hospital, and—and it seems rather silly to go on a honeymoon when we've already been married two months,' she added lamely, evading his suddenly concerned gaze.

She couldn't stand his concern, not when his night-time ramblings about another woman had broken her heart!

'Every woman should have a honeymoon she can look back on,' he gently reproved her lack of enthusiasm.

'And who told you that?' she said sharply, embarrassed colour darkening her cheeks as Justin raised his brows in surprise at her vehemence.

'Darling, I married you so quickly, you didn't have time to arrange the grand wedding you must have really wanted. At least let me give you the honeymoon,' he softly cajoled.

'I'm really not interested in going away at the moment.' She picked up her napkin from her lap to fold it precisely and place it next to the cup of coffee which was all she had had for breakfast. 'We've very busy on the ward, and——'

'Caroline, what's wrong?' Justin's hand clasped hers as it still rested on the table. 'You've been very jumpy the last three days. I thought you would welcome the idea of some time away——'

'And so you decided to indulge me!' she flared resentfully, glaring at him. 'I'm not a child, Justin, who has to be spoilt and petted when I fall down and graze my knee! I'm a trained nurse, responsible for people's lives; I certainly don't expect my husband to treat me like a moron!'

Justin gave a pained wince. 'I see one of the other characteristics of a pregnant woman is surfacing,' he said drily.

Her eyes flashed. 'And what's that?'

He shrugged. 'The uncertain temper.'

'And just how would you know?' she challenged, pulling her hand away from his as she stood up. 'I do not want a honeymoon, either now or in the future. And now, if you'll excuse me, I have to go to work.'

'No, I won't.'

She turned sharply at the door to the dining-room at his softly spoken words. 'No, you won't what?' she prompted impatiently.

He stood up slowly, towering over her as he joined her at the door. 'No, I won't excuse you,' he told her firmly, his hand under her chin as he made her look up at him.

'Caro——'

'Don't you dare!' she cried vehemently, wrenching away from him. 'Don't you dare try and seduce me, you—you——'

'Caroline, for God's sake, what is the matter with you?' He lost all patience with her seemingly unreasonable behaviour.

'I'm going to work.' She threw open the door. 'I don't want to talk about this any more!'

She ran out into the hallway, rushing past a wide-eyed Mrs Avery on her way to see if they wanted more coffee, and, grabbing her jacket off the hall-stand, hurried from the apartment as if she were being pursued.

She heartily thanked the fact that nursing didn't give a lot of time for private thought as she somehow managed to get through the morning without a crack in her well-formed defences showing. But by lunch-time she felt drained, both physically and mentally, and, ignoring the hungry cry of her stomach, she went for a walk outside, where she hoped the freshness of the day would help to clear her head.

The hospital grounds were lovely, kept that way by the full-time gardeners they employed, although the beauty of the flowers didn't reach her today, her thoughts immediately returning to that scene between herself and Justin this morning. She was behaving like a shrew, she knew that, and yet his suggestion of a honeymoon had just seemed to be the final straw.

For three days she had done her best to pretend that everything was as it had always been between them, that Justin didn't call out for another woman in his sleep, but this morning she just hadn't been able to pretend any more!

She had accepted so much from Justin because she loved him and wanted to be with him: the fact that he couldn't love her, that he didn't want their baby; she just felt she had come to the end of the disillusionment she could take and still love him that unquestioningly.

'Slow down! For God's sake, Caroline, I'm not

as young as I was, and I'm not sure you should be walking at that pace in your condition!'

She turned to find Tony hurrying after her, panting with the effort of trying to catch her up. One look at the man she would have married if she had never met Justin, one look at his uncomplicated face, and the tears she had been repressing all morning burst out in a flood, her body racked by deep sobs.

'Hey, women don't usually cry as soon as they see me,' he gently rebuked as he took her into his arms, Caroline's tears instantly wetting both of them. 'Caroline, what on earth has happened?' he demanded in a concerned voice.

She just cried all the harder, burying her face in his white coat.

'Has something happened to Justin?' he prompted worriedly.

She let out a loud wail before burying her face in his coat again.

'Caroline, we'll have to go somewhere more private if you're going to carry on like this,' he warned with feeling.

She roused herself enough to look around them, realising as she did so that these gardens were visible from several of the wards. 'Get me away from here!' she groaned in embarrassment.

With his arm about her shoulders to shield her from prying eyes, Tony took her to one of the private lounges, shooing out the only other occupant, a student nurse, so that they could be completely alone.

He sat down in a chair with her on his lap. 'Now tell me what's wrong,' he encouraged gently, removing her crumpled cap so that she could be more comfortable against his shoulder.

'You were right, Tony,' she sniffled self-pityingly. 'You warned me I could never hold Justin's interest——'

'I didn't exactly say that,' he denied uncomfortably. 'Anyway, I was angry that night; I said things in the heat of temper.'

'And sometimes they can be all too truthful,' she sobbed.

'Have the two of you argued?' Tony guessed with some relief. 'I shouldn't worry about it. Sonia and I do it all the time, and the making up can be——'

'Justin has someone else,' she told him flatly.

'What?'

She swallowed hard, still shaking quite badly. 'Justin is in love with someone else,' she stated much more calmly than she felt.

'No.' Tony shook his head.

She gave a start of surprise, blinking dazedly at his absolute certainty she was wrong. 'He has another woman, Tony,' she insisted firmly. 'I even know her name,' she added shakily.

'From where?' he prompted patiently.

'From his dreams,' she answered defensively. Somehow she had expected Tony to sympathise with her, to be her ally, not to have him flatly refuse to believe in Justin's duplicity. 'He calls her name in his dreams!'

'Oh, well, that doesn't mean anything,' Tony scorned. 'I dream about——well, never mind who I dream about,' he dismissed ruefully. 'But I can tell you I usually want to do more than talk to her!'

Caroline shook her head. 'This isn't that sort of dream, Tony,' she said confidently. 'Justin cares for this woman. Very much.'

'I don't believe it. I'm sorry.' He held up his hands defensively as she stood up to frown down at him. 'I may still think he did a dirty thing by making my girlfriend fall in love with him,' he grimaced, 'but I can say with all honesty that I don't believe he's interested in any other woman but you. You can't really believe otherwise, Caroline,' he rebuked. 'Have you asked him about this woman?'

She turned away. Asking Justin about Penny was the one thing she had put off doing—she was afraid of the answer. Once she knew, irrevocably, that he loved someone else, she wouldn't be able to stay with him, no matter how much she might love him.

'No, I can't; don't you see that?' She looked at Tony anxiously.

He shook his head. 'I can see that you're probably putting yourself through a lot of unnecessary pain.' He sighed. 'Caroline, I have the most reason to want to believe Justin is an out and out bastard, to have you leave him, but the truth of the matter is I like the man, I respect his honesty, and I truly don't believe he would stay married to you if he were in love with someone else.'

'Even if that someone were unnattainable?' she questioned uncertainly.

'Even then,' Tony confirmed. 'Damn it, Caroline, the night of my parents' anniversary party he was dating my sister; by the end of the evening he had told her he no longer wanted to see her because he wanted you. He isn't a man to mince his words, or his emotions, and if he wanted this other woman he would have told you—and her.'

She still looked uncertain, wanting to believe what he said was the truth, but the memory of the way Justin cried out the other woman's name kept haunting her; he was like a man in torment.

'Caroline, if it really distresses you that much then ask him about her,' Tony advised impatiently. 'But don't keep letting the thing fester and grow in your mind.'

She gave him a wan smile. 'I'll think about it. You know, you aren't bad as a brother.' She bent down to kiss him on the cheek.

'Caroline,' drawled a pleasant voice. 'Tony?' Justin added questioningly. 'And please, don't either of you say "this isn't what it seems",' he murmured derisively as they both turned to him with stricken faces. 'What it "seems" couldn't possibly be taking place here!' He looked pointedly around the lounge that anyone could walk into at any moment—and had!

Tony stood up. 'I'm glad you said that,' he said with some relief. 'I might have found it a little difficult explaining to Sonia what I did to merit having you put me in one of my own wards!'

Justin gave the ghost of a smile, his gaze bleak. 'I try never to jump to conclusions,' he bit out harshly. 'So what *were* you doing?' He looked at them both coldly.

All Caroline could do was stare at him; Justin was the last person she had expected to see here today. Oh, he knew his way around here OK, had sought her out several times when he was trying to persuade her to go out with him, but what was he doing here now, and looking as if he hadn't been to work, wearing a casual grey shirt and denims that hugged his waist and thighs? She never failed to receive a jolt of physical awareness whenever she saw him in clothes like this, and today was no exception.

'I——'

'Aren't pregnant women emotional?' Tony cut in dismissively to the other man. 'All my medical training and I never realised they all fall apart at the seams. I'm going to make sure Sonia knows exactly what she's letting herself in for before she gets pregnant,' he grimaced. 'I don't fancy walking around damp from tears all the time.' He pulled his damp jacket away from him pointedly. 'And the slightest little thing sets them off.' He shook his head disgustedly. 'I only told Caroline I thought she should slow down a little and she started blubbering all over me. Very embarrassing, I can tell you,' he confided in Justin.

He was doing his best to smooth things over for her, and at that moment Caroline could have kissed him all over again. Only she very wisely didn't!

'Don't worry, Tony,' Justin drawled. 'The only person Caroline will be ''blubbering'' all over in future is me.' He turned to her, complete awareness of the real situation in his gaze, although he said nothing. 'I've come to take you out to lunch,' he told her softly.

Her eyes widened, and then she gave a groan of disappointment as she looked down at her fob-watch. 'I've got to be back on duty in a few minutes,' she said regretfully.

'Hm,' he murmured, looking pointedly at the other man. 'If you'll excuse us . . .'

Tony grinned. 'You know, you dismiss a man even better then my old tutor used to—and he was an expert!'

'Thank you.' Justin gave an acknowledging smile.

Tony winked at Caroline before leaving, his tuneless whistle echoing up the corridor seconds later.

'You know,' Justin spoke softly, 'in a way I regret what I did to him two months ago.'

Caroline frowned; he regretted marrying her?

'No,' he mocked her unspoken question. 'I don't regret marrying you, only that I had to hurt Tony to do it. But I think he and your sister are going to make it, don't you?' he prompted lightly.

She didn't trust his calmly pleasant mood, was sure he must really be angry at finding her and Tony in such a compromising situation; he had to be biding his time before making his displeasure felt.

'I think so,' she answered his question, sure from the amount of times Sonia entered Tony's conversation that he did really care for her sister. 'Justin, just now really wasn't what it seemed.' She decided that attack was the best form of defence.

'On reflection,' he drawled slowly, 'it seemed like an old friend giving comfort because you were upset. Wasn't that what it was?'

'Yes,' she challenged, picking up her crumpled cap from the small coffee-table beside the chair she and Tony had been sitting in, staring down at it as she waited for Justin's icy anger to wash over her.

'And *I* was the reason you were upset,' he said softly.

Her head went back, her eyes wide as she stared at him. 'Yes,' she confirmed tremulously.

He drew in a ragged breath. 'I'm sorry, I've been—preoccupied the last few days,' his voice was gruff.

He was as aware as she that that preoccupation included not making love to her, not even touching her unless it was accidentally.

Justin sighed at her lack of response. 'I've had—something on my mind. Will you let me make it up to you?' he urged gently.

Caroline frowned. How could he possibly make up to her the fact that he talked of another woman in his sleep, that he spoke of her with love?

And yet this man, his gaze soft, his mouth curved into a gentle smile, wasn't the same man

who had so cold-bloodedly asked her to marry
him. That man had been cold himself, his emotions
firmly held in check, only relaxing his rigid control
when they were in bed together. The Justin
standing in front of her now was the same man she
loved when he made love to her, except they
weren't in bed. She didn't know what it meant,
after the last three days she was afraid to even
hope, but surely it had to mean something?

She swallowed hard. 'How?'

His gaze warmed even more. 'By first of all
taking you out to lunch——'

'I told you,' she groaned. 'I have to be back on
duty in a few minutes.' She shook her head.

'And if you recall I said "hm",' he teased. 'Are
you going to be angry if I tell you that I haven't
just arranged for you to take the rest of the day off
but the next eight days as well, that as you couldn't
seem to make your mind up about a honeymoon
I've made it up for you?' He eyed her
questioningly.

Angry because she didn't have to come to work
for a week and try to put a brave face on things?
Angry that she was going to be alone with Justin
for that time and possibly straighten out the
tension between them? Angry that he had cared
enough to behave so arrogantly?

'Caroline?' he prompted with a pained wince.

'Ordinarily I would be very angry at your
arrogance,' she told him abruptly. 'Ordinarily I
might even have told you what you could do with
it. But then,' she added lightly, 'pregnant women

aren't "ordinary"! When do we leave? And where are we going?'

His expression had changed only slightly as she mentioned the baby she carried, and he tried to mask even that, only Caroline's extreme sensitivity on the subject making it obvious to her.

'We leave as soon as you've been home to change,' he said briskly. 'Mrs Avery is even now doing your packing for you. As to where we're going, that's to be a surprise, but I will tell you, just so that you aren't disappointed, that you aren't going to need your passport.'

'That's good.' Her eyes glowed with laughter. 'Because I don't have one!'

'You don't?' Justin laughed in disbelief. 'Then thank God I didn't whisk you off to the Bahamas as I first intended. I only decided against it because seven days isn't long enough to get over the jet-lag and start enjoying yourself. We'll have to do something about getting you a passport, Caroline,' he told her as they left the lounge on their way out of the hospital. 'Who knows what I might arrange for Christmas!'

The woman called Penny still stood between them, perhaps she always would, but Caroline couldn't resist this Justin, a light-hearted, indulgently teasing Justin—and perhaps she didn't want to!

She felt as excited as a child as Justin put their luggage in the boot of the car. But they hadn't been driving for more than half an hour when Justin turned into a small car park.

'I never did give you lunch,' he reminded her ruefully as she looked at him enquiringly.

It was a delightful country inn, authentic by the look of the low beamed ceiling; Caroline chuckled as Justin had to bend his head not to crash into the beams.

They had never done any of the things other newly married couples had, no drives out into the country, no quiet lunches together in quiet inns like this one, no walking along a beach hand in hand——She brought herself to an abrupt halt on the last image; she just couldn't imagine Justin on a beach, getting his trousers damp and sand in his shoes! But then she hadn't married any ordinary man, and she had known that when she fell in love with him.

And she didn't feel that Penny was with them now. It was as if Justin had left his thoughts of the other woman behind in London, that the woman no longer intruded on their relationship. Oh, God, she hoped so!

They dined on typical bar fare, indulging Caroline's sweet tooth afterwards with a huge bowl of trifle.

She gave a sigh of satisfaction as they emerged out into the sunshine. 'That was wonderful!' A shadow clouded her eyes. 'Er—have you been there before?' She couldn't bear the thought of being with him in the same places Penny had.

'No.' He turned on the ignition. 'Just a lucky guess.'

'Oh, yes,' she beamed at him, leaning back

against the head-rest. 'I think I could fall asleep now.' She laughed.

'Then why don't you?' Justin tuned the radio into a station playing softly romantic music. 'We still have quite a way to go.'

She didn't mean to fall asleep at all, meant to enjoy every moment of being with this man who was making her fall more and more in love with him by the minute, but three virtually sleepless nights, the warmth of the day, and the soft music all resulted in her being asleep within minutes of their resuming their journey.

She only woke up when Justin brought the car to a halt. Sitting up to look dazedly about her, she saw that they were parked in front of an old manor house that was approached by a long gravel drive that wound through picturesque gardens, the house itself old and beautifully maintained, the whole place having an unreal appearance about it.

She turned curiously to Justin as he sat watching her reaction.

'It is a hotel,' he assured her, turning to smile at the doorman as he opened the car door. 'We'll be there in a moment,' he instructed distantly. 'If you could see that our luggage is taken to our room. Mr and Mrs de Wolfe,' he supplied as he handed the keys to the car boot to the other man.

'But where are we?' Caroline demanded excitedly as she looked at the beauty around her, the immaculate gardens that seemed to go on for ever, the mellow grace of the manor house.

'Devon,' Justin supplied indulgently, enjoying

her pleasure in their surroundings. 'This place probably once belonged to a member of the aristocracy who fell on hard times. Whatever the reason, it's now a hotel.'

'It's lovely.' She stepped out of the car as he held her door open for her.

'So are you.' His gaze darkened as he looked down at her. 'Are you feeling rested now?' he prompted in a husky voice.

'After all that sleep, I should hope so!' she dismissed ruefully.

'Good,' he murmured as he clasped her elbow, and they walked up the steps together. 'Because when I requested our suite here I intended it should be a honeymoon in the full sense of the word.'

When Caroline saw the four-poster bed that took up most of their bedroom, she knew exactly what he 'intended'!

CHAPTER SEVEN

'I'M SURE the waiter thought we were newlyweds,' Caroline chuckled as the two of them entered their suite later that evening. 'He started to offer me confetti instead of dessert!'

Justin smiled, darkly handsome in his tailored evening suit. 'We are newlyweds; two months doesn't exactly make us a staid married couple.'

Caroline laughed happily, feeling more light-hearted tonight than she ever had before. 'I don't think coming up to bed at nine-thirty dented the impression!'

Justin put the keys to their suite on the low drinks cabinet. 'I only got through until that time because you insisted on having coffee,' he drawled, throwing off his jacket, and loosening his bow-tie.

She leant into his body as she unfastened the top button of his shirt for him. 'When you made the booking here did you check that they do room-service?' she murmured throatily. 'Because I have the distinct impression that Devon is going to be wasted on us!'

'I checked.' He curved her tightly against him, making her aware of every hard muscle in his body. 'It's a twenty-four hour service, just in case we lose track of time,' he murmured before feasting on her

119

mouth.

Three days without his kisses and caresses made Caroline's response all the more fiery, her fingers clenched in his hair as she more than returned his passion.

'Oh, Justin, I've missed you,' she groaned as his lips moved feveredly down her throat.

'I'm sorry, darling. So sorry. I never meant——'

'Just love me, Justin,' she urged with feeling. 'Just love me as if you'll never let me go.'

He became suddenly tense, raising his head to look at her. 'I never will let you go, Caro,' he ground out fiercely. 'Never!'

She could see the savage pride of possession in his gaze, knew that he meant every word. Penny was losing and she was winning! Maybe *that* was why the other woman had been on his mind so much lately; his subconscious had already been saying goodbye to that other love, allowing Caroline into his heart instead. Oh, he still hadn't said the words, and perhaps he never would, but he was different with her now, and it could only be because he had come to care for her in spite of himself. What had started out as a depressing day now seemed full of possibilities.

'Then love me, Justin,' she encouraged with a slight sob in her voice. 'Love me!'

Even his lovemaking was different tonight, just as fiercely intense, more so after the last three nights of loneliness, but tonight he was intent on pleasing her as never before, raising her again and again to the heights only to deny her release at the last possible moment.

Caroline felt as if she were going insane as he once again denied her, moving restlessly against him, finally unable to bear his slow, tormenting caresses any longer, becoming the aggressor as she pushed him down beneath her, the one to do the possessing, controlling their passion, and Justin, until they both reached a shuddering release.

She lay exhausted against his chest, their bodies clinging together damply, their breathing moving in ragged harmony.

'I always wondered what it must feel like to be ravaged by a woman,' Justin murmured lazily into the silence.

Cheeks warm with embarrassment, Caroline lifted her head to look at him, reassured by the sated satisfaction in his face. 'And?' she teased throatily.

'And——' he stretched like a contented kitten, almost dislodging Caroline from her more than comfortable position above him '——I think I might grow to like it.' He grinned up at her.

Her face burnt from the deliberate provocation of his remark. 'Justin de Wolfe, you are——'

'Uh-uh, I know you aren't really angry with me,' he said languidly. 'What was it Tony said about your sister? When she's really angry she launches into his full name!'

'Justin David James Charles de Wolfe is too much of a mouthful for anyone—let alone when I'm feeling so very tired.' She watched him beneath lowered lashes.

His brows rose in disappointment. 'Not too tired, I hope; this *is* supposed to be the first night of our honeymoon.'

'Oh, I think I might manage to find a little more strength from somewhere,' she teased him. 'Of course, if you're going to let me do all the work again . . .'

'My darling Caro——' he rolled over so that she lay beneath him '——this time you won't have to do anything but just lie there and——'

'Justin David James Charles de Wolfe!' She frowned warningly, rewarded by his throaty chuckle. 'Have you ever known me to "just lie there"?'

'No,' he said with satisfaction. 'It isn't in that passionate nature of yours. But I do think we should at least try the bed out once while we're here, don't you?' he added derisively.

For the first time she realised that, as on that first night together, they had made it no further than the carpeted floor, this time in the beautifully decorated and furnished lounge to their suite.

She smiled up at Justin. 'I think everyone should make love in a four-poster bed at least once in their lives.'

Justin looked around the room appreciatively. 'I suppose there are endless possibilities for the rest of our stay here.' He stood up, lifting her up easily into his arms. 'But right now the experience of a lifetime awaits us!'

Devon definitely was wasted on them this time around; they rarely left their suite, and when they did it was only to walk on the beach they discovered on walking down a cliff-path at the back of the hotel. To Caroline's surprise Justin enjoyed nothing better than taking off his shoes and socks, rolling up his trousers, and paddling in the surf with her at these times.

It was as if she was seeing yet another Justin, an even more endearing one, an infinitely more loveable one. And, when she already felt as if she loved him to bursting point, that seemed impossible—yet it was happening. Never more so than on the last day of their stay when she awoke to the worst feelings of nausea she had ever experienced.

The nausea didn't really hit her until she moved away from Justin's sleeping body, intending to use the bathroom before he even woke up. As soon as she stepped out of bed, the feelings of sickness washed over her in waves, and she swayed unsteadily on her feet as she tried to swallow down the feeling. Realising she wasn't going to be able to do that, she made a mad dash for the bathroom before she disgraced herself all over the luxuriously expensive carpet!

Her stomach kept heaving even once it was empty, and tears streamed down her face. Morning sickness! How were she and Justin going to carry on as if nothing was changing in their marriage when she couldn't even lift her head off the pillow in the mornings? The tears began to fall even harder.

'It's nothing to cry about.' Justin was suddenly

at her side, bathing her face, soothing her. 'Come on back to bed,' he encouraged gently. 'I'll get you some tea and dry toast sent up. Or would you prefer biscuits?' All the time he was talking he helped her back into the bedroom, tucking her in firmly beneath the covers before going to the telephone and placing their order.

All the time he spoke on the telephone, Caroline watched him miserably over the top of the bedclothes, sure her morning sickness had ruined what had been a perfect honeymoon so far.

'They're sure to realise why you asked for dry toast,' she sniffled miserably once Justin was off the telephone.

Smiling gently, he came to sit on the side of the bed, careful not to pull the covers tightly across her sensitive stomach. 'What difference does it make?' he cajoled, bathing her face once again.

'They're all going to think—going to think—'

'That we can't keep our hands off each other,' he teased softly. 'Besides, *we* know we've really been married two months, and that the baby is perfectly legitimate.'

She swallowed hard. 'That's the first time you've mentioned the baby without—wincing.' She looked up at him searchingly.

His gaze lost all its humour, suddenly evasive. 'Caroline, I——' He broke off as a knock sounded on the door, and stood up with what seemed to Caroline to be relief. 'That will be our breakfast,' he said lightly. 'Just stay where you are and I'll bring it through to you.'

As if she was going to go anywhere in her condition! Oh, damn it! Being bad-tempered about this wasn't going to help the situation at all. Justin couldn't help not wanting the baby, and she couldn't help her morning sickness either. She would just have to put a brave face on it if she weren't to make him impatient with the whole thing.

She was attempting to sit up against the pillows when Justin came back into the room with the breakfast tray.

He frowned as he saw what she was trying to do. 'I told you to stay where you were,' he reproved, putting the tray down to cross the room to her side.

She forced a bright smile to her lips, not realising it came out looking more like a grimace against her pallor. 'I'm feeling much better——'

'Like hell you are,' his voice rasped. 'Don't be a damned fool. Get back down in that bed before I decide to put you over my knee instead!' He settled her back down.

She frowned up at him from the lying position he had gently, but firmly, pushed her into. 'Stop swearing at me,' she said in a disgruntled voice.

'That isn't easy to do when you're behaving irresponsibly,' he scowled. 'You look like hell, you obviously feel even worse, and you have the nerve to try and tell me you're feeling better!'

The tears threatened to overflow again. 'I was only——'

'I know what "you were only".' He sat on the side of the bed again. 'Darling, you're my wife, and when you feel unwell, whatever the circumstances, I want to know about it,' he told her abruptly. 'You don't have to put on some sort of act with me, as if you're afraid to admit to feeling ill.' His gaze darkened as she gave a guilty blush. 'I'm not some sort of ogre, Caroline.' He stood up to move away from her. 'Now drink your tea and chew on your toast,' he encouraged gently as he handed them to her. 'You'll start to feel better in no time.'

She didn't exactly make a miraculous recovery, and as she fought down the nausea for the rest of the day, she had a feeling her sickness wasn't going to be confined to just the morning, but Justin was marvellous with her, knowing exactly the right moment to sit down and take a rest, or hand her one of the biscuits they had gone into the nearest town to buy. But he never again alluded to the fact that her sickness was caused by her pregnancy, once again ignoring its existence.

When she turned to him that night he gently took her in his arms and just held her against him, the caress of his hand on her back soothing rather than arousing.

She looked up at him with shyly encouraging eyes. 'I really am feeling much better now,' she assured him truthfully. 'And I'd hate to waste the last night of our honeymoon,' she added enticingly.

His gaze was searching. 'It isn't going to be wasted if we just hold each other,' he finally told her gently, obviously not satisfied with what he saw in her face.

'But I don't want to just hold you,' she protested impatiently. 'I really am all right, Justin,' she added enticingly, playing with the dark swirls of hair on his chest, knowing by the sudden unevenness of his breathing that it was having the desired effect. 'I have the feeling I'm going to be a night person with this pregnancy,' she said happily.

Justin's arms closed about her. 'How fortunate,' he murmured with satisfaction before his mouth claimed hers and all conversation ceased.

Their honeymoon had changed their relationship yet again. Justin seemed more relaxed with her than ever, and while he didn't openly mention her pregnancy again he was very considerate of her condition, always managing to waken before her so that he could bring her the tea and dry toast in bed. Usually this managed to ease the nausea, which seemed to be lessening as her pregnancy progressed anyway. By the time she was three months pregnant the sickness had stopped completely, something Caroline was more than grateful for.

Their social life had picked up, too, in recent weeks; they saw Sonia and Tony often, going out to the theatre and dinner occasionally, too. But Don Lindford hadn't called again, and when Caroline asked Justin if he had managed to contact the other man he had muttered something about him being out of the country at the moment.

It was on a return invitation to Sonia and Tony's one evening that the first moments of awkwardness since their holiday occurred. The last five weeks had been such happy ones, her relationship with Justin closer than ever. He no longer dreamt about the woman called Penny, or called out for her in the night, so Caroline could only assume that her guess at Justin fighting to hold on to that old love had been the right one; and that Justin had lost. The woman Penny was out of his mind and out of his heart now; she was sure of that.

But as soon as she saw that Sonia and Tony's other guests for dinner were Paula and a handsome blond-haired man, she knew that the evening wasn't going to go as smoothly and as pleasantly as she had hoped when she and Justin had set out earlier.

'I hear congratulations are in order,' Paula drawled as soon as they had been introduced to the man who was her partner for the evening, Brian Pendleton seeming to be a pleasant man.

'Thank you,' Caroline accepted abruptly, wary of the other woman on this, their first meeting since the night she and Justin had met for the first time.

'I can't say I exactly envy you,' the other woman mocked. 'Waddling around the place for the next few months!' She ran her hands pointedly over the perfect smoothness of her waist, very beautiful in a blue and silver gown that showed more silver as she moved.

Caroline opened her mouth to make a cutting reply, looking up at Justin as his arm came possessively about her waist.

He smiled at her encouragingly. 'Caroline is much too graceful to ever "waddle" anywhere,' he derided.

Paula gave a bitchy smile. 'You mean you'll still love her when she's so rounded with your child that you can scarcely share a bed!'

Justin's gaze hardened. 'There will never be a time that Caroline and I don't share a bed, Paula,' he told her softly, a warning in his voice.

The older woman's mouth tightened resentfully, but she was wise enough to say no more on the subject.

The evening was completely ruined for Caroline; how could she relax and enjoy herself when Paula Hammond seemed determined to make sure she didn't? Not that she could blame the other woman for still being upset about the way Justin had ended their relationship, but it had been five months ago, and Justin was very much the married man now.

'I'm sorry,' Sonia groaned, having asked Caroline to help her in the kitchen so that the two of them could talk alone. 'She more or less invited herself once she knew you and Justin were coming tonight, and Paula has enough arrogance for ten women!' she added with feeling. 'I would have put you off, but in the circumstances that might have looked too obvious.'

'It's all right.' Caroline squeezed her arm, seeing that her sister was really upset about the situation. 'I don't have anything to fear from Paula,' she said confidently, sure of Justin in a way that a woman like Paula could never make her doubt.

'Except her tongue!' Sonia reminded her drily. 'I feel sorry for poor Brian Pendleton; he's obviously only been brought along as an afterthought. Tony is absolutely disgusted by Paula's behaviour.' Sonia sighed. 'That's all we need to complete the evening: the two of them having one of their not unfamous arguments!'

Caroline chuckled softly. 'Justin could act as referee!'

Her sister nodded absently. 'I'm not even sure I have enough food; Paula only invited herself an hour ago.'

'You always cook too much anyway,' Caroline assured her lightly. 'I doubt if any of us will go hungry.'

Sonia squeezed her eyes tightly shut. 'I can't believe Paula actually publicly challenged your place in Justin's bed,' she groaned disbelievingly, shaking her head. 'Anyone with any sense—and that seems to exclude Paula in this case—can clearly see he can't take his eyes off you.'

Caroline laughed softly, warmed by the knowledge. 'Please don't worry about it; I'm not going to.' And surprisingly she knew that she wasn't, these few minutes she took to collect herself renewing her confidence in the marriage she and Justin were trying to build together. Nothing a woman like Paula Hammond could say could damage the relationship they already had together.

Her smile was completely natural as she went back into the lounge, sitting on the arm of Justin's chair as she leant into him, looking up to meet

Paula's scathing glance with questioningly raised brows.

'Isn't it perfectly nauseous to observe newly-weds together?' Paula spoke drily to no one in particular. 'But then I suppose you know all about nausea at the moment, don't you, Caroline?' she prompted with a sweetness that didn't fool anyone—and wasn't supposed to!

'Paula——'

'Actually,' Caroline cut across Tony's anger with an apologetic smile in his direction, 'I'm feeling in the best of health,' she told the other woman derisively. 'But then that's as it should be when I'm feeling so happy,' she added challengingly.

Paula gave a disgusted snort, but was prevented from further comment by Sonia's firm announcement that dinner was ready.

Caroline smiled at Justin as they took their seats, but although he returned the smile she could see from the anger in his gaze that he was at the end of his patience where Paula was concerned.

Paula hadn't got where she was in her profession by not being able to read people, and as they ate dinner she chatted amiably with them all, just as if her bitchiness had never occurred.

Caroline shared a conspiratorial smile with Tony, could see by his grimace that he could cheerfully have strangled his sister if he had been allowed to.

It wasn't until they were all sitting together in the living-room, drinking coffee, that Paula's self-control lapsed once again.

'Isn't this all very civilised?' Again she spoke to no one in particular. 'My brother is married to the sister of the woman he once intended marrying, and that sister is married to the man I——'

'You what, Paula?' Justin prompted in a dangerously soft voice.

Her eyes flashed deeply green. 'Whom I admire very much,' she answered challengingly.

'The professional admiration is reciprocated,' he bit out. 'Otherwise you wouldn't be working for my law firm.'

Paula flushed angrily at the veiled threat. 'I was only pointing out how curious it is that Tony should now be married to Caroline's sister instead of Caroline!'

'Not curious at all—when you consider the fact that he happens to be in love with Sonia,' Justin grated harshly.

'As you are in love with Caroline?' the self-assured woman taunted.

Some of the colour left Caroline's cheeks. She had never dared to openly voice that question, and she knew Justin would deeply resent a third person intruding in this familiar way. She could only hope he wouldn't deny the emotion in his chilling anger!

'Paula, why don't you go home?' Tony burst out furiously. 'You've done some stupid things in your time, but this must surely rate as the stupidest!'

His sister's eyes flashed again. 'You——'

'More coffee, anyone?' Sonia broke in brightly.

Paula wasn't to be put off. 'You——'

'No?' Sonia continued as if no one had spoken. 'In that case it's time for the part everyone dreads; washing-up! Paula,' she spoke coldly, 'you can come and help me.'

Surprised brows rose over mockingly appreciative green eyes. 'So the little mouse can roar,' Paula drawled, standing up.

'She can do more than roar,' Sonia told her sweetly, 'so don't push it, hm?' Her saccharine smile matched her tone.

Paula gave a huskily appreciative laugh. 'What a lot of champions you have, Caroline,' she said softly. 'Obviously "roaring" isn't a family characteristic. But then, of course, it wouldn't be; the two of you aren't really sisters, are you?' she dismissed with a shrug. 'Poor Caroline; first Sonia superseded you with the people you considered your parents, and then she came along and took the man in your life, too.' She gave a feigned sigh. 'Life can sometimes be such a bitch, can't it?'

'Not half such a bitch as you!' Tony sprang angrily to his feet. 'For your information, Caroline finished with me long before I first went out with Sonia,' he bit out contemptuously. 'And Caroline has always been her parents' much-loved eldest daughter. Now you can take yourself, and the poor man who is stuck with you for the evening——' he gave Brian Pendleton a pitying glance '—and get out of my home,' he told his sister harshly.

Furious green eyes turned on Caroline and Justin as Caroline once again sat on the arm of his chair.

'You don't need to tell me to get out of my office, too,' Paula rasped. 'I couldn't go on working there, anyway, watching you make such a fool of yourself over a woman who obviously knows a meal-ticket when she sees one.' She gave a scornful laugh as Caroline paled. 'She even made sure of it by getting pregnant straight away. But can you ever be sure it isn't my brother's baby?' Her head went back in challenge.

Caroline was barely aware of the shocked gasps around the room. She stared at Justin, a coldly furious Justin that she had never seen before, a nerve pulsing in his jaw as he slowly stood up.

'If you'll excuse me?' He spoke softly to their host, receiving a nod from the still-stunned Tony. Justin reached the door in two strides and wrenched it open, his silver gaze ripping into a now pale Paula as she realised, by the fact that she had succeeded in infuriating a man who could usually remain calm through any situation, that she had finally gone too far. 'Don't come near either Caroline or myself—but especially Caroline —again, or I'm not going to be answerable for the consequences. Do I make myself clear?'

'Very.' Paula picked up her clutch-bag with a calmness that defied him to think his threat meant anything to her. And maybe it would have looked convincing if her hand hadn't been trembling so badly. 'Come along, Brian,' she instructed haughtily.

The slenderly handsome man stood slowly to his

feet. 'I'll see you to your car,' he nodded politely.

Green eyes widened. 'But I drove you here,' she reminded lightly.

He nodded. 'I'll see you to your car,' he repeated tautly.

The three left sitting in the room, once Paula and the not-so-amenable Brian Pendleton had left, all looked shattered by the vitriolic attack, Justin standing beside the lounge door, breathing deeply in his anger.

Tony was the first to recover. 'My God, I didn't realise she was capable——I hope you don't believe there was any truth in that wild accusation she made about the baby.' He shook his head. 'Because it *was* wild,' he insisted firmly. 'Caroline and I never—we never——'

She was barely conscious of Justin's, 'I'm well aware of that,' although she was grateful for it, had hoped Paula's provocative taunt wouldn't make him reconsider the initial doubts he had had about the baby being his.

'Caroline.' Suddenly Justin appeared in her line of vision as she stared down at the floor; he was down on his haunches in front of her. 'Darling, it's all over now,' he soothed gently, pushing her hair back from her forehead.

'She was right,' she said in a pained voice, looking up at Justin with bewildered eyes. 'For years I've denied it, but—but I always felt pushed out by the fact that my parents had children of their own. I just——No one has ever put it into words before.' She shook her head.

She could see an emotion much like love in his eyes as he moved forward to pull her head down against his shoulder. 'Darling, of course you felt that way,' he said understandingly. 'Any four-year-old would feel resentment, let alone one who had been brought up to believe she was special because she was adopted.' His hands moved caressingly across her back.

She blinked back the tears. 'But I felt that way again when Sonia married Tony. I didn't love him myself, I—I just didn't like the idea of her marrying him.' She turned to her sister, pain etched into her face. 'I'm sorry. I—I'm sorry.' She could no longer hold back the tears.

'Caroline, you have nothing to feel sorry for,' Sonia chided gently, at her side, too, now. 'Do you think I didn't realise how you felt? God, in your place I would have refused to have anything to do with Simon and me. But you didn't, you were like a second little mother to us.' She smiled at the memory. 'And if you had even once guessed how I felt about Tony before the two of you finished you would probably have backed out and let me have him! Caroline, you don't have a selfish bone in your body, and we all love you.'

Years of hiding a resentment she had thought no one else knew about were suddenly stripped from her, leaving her free in a way she had never known before. Until Sonia and Simon were born she had known she was a very special person in her parents' life, but once she knew there was to be a baby of their own, even worse, *two* babies together, she had never felt as secure of their love again, had spent the rest of her life trying to prove herself to them. And now she saw it wasn't necessary. Sonia was right; all of her family did love her.

She gave a wan smile. 'You're right, Tony.' She smiled at him over Sonia's head. 'Pregnant women are much too emotional.'

He returned the smile affectionately. 'I think this pregnant woman's emotionalism was long overdue,' he said gently.

She turned back to Justin, warmed by the concern in his gaze. 'Paula must have wanted you very much, to have risked everything in that way,' she said sadly.

'Not really,' his mouth twisted. 'She had already handed in her notice, and was due to leave at the end of the month.'

'That's Paula all over,' Tony dismissed disgustedly. 'Even her "grand gesture" turns out to be not quite what it seemed.'

The touch of humour lightened the atmosphere, and they all smiled a little with relief at the passing of the awkwardness Paula had so wantonly caused.

'I think we should leave now.' Justin straightened up.

Caroline shook her head. 'I'll help Sonia with the clearing away first.'

'Don't be silly,' her sister dismissed lightly. 'Tony can help me do that.'

'Yes,' he grimaced, 'I can help her do that.'

Caroline was completely poised again now, and she stood up with a shake of her head. 'You two men enjoy a brandy together while Sonia and I tackle the washing-up.'

'I——'

'That sounds like a good idea,' Justin agreed firmly, deftly cutting off the other man's protest, sharing a look of complete understanding with Caroline as he realised she wanted to talk to her sister alone before they left. 'Make mine a large one.' He scowled, sitting down, stretching his long legs out in front of him in a completely relaxed pose.

As soon as the kitchen door closed behind them Sonia and Caroline were in each other's arms.

'I never realised—— I thought I was very ungrateful—— Do Mummy and Daddy know?' Caroline groaned at what a fool she had been all her life.

'I'm sure they know how you felt, yes,' Sonia nodded emotionally. 'But they knew you would feel worse if they spoke to you about it. Do you know that when we were younger Simon and I always envied you? Yes, we did,' she insisted at Caroline's sceptical look. 'We never thought it was fair that you had been especially chosen by Mummy and Daddy and we had just been born to them!' her sister told her ruefully. 'It was only when we got older that we realised perhaps you didn't see it that way.'

She shook her head. 'I suppose children always want what isn't theirs; I wanted to *be* Mum and Dad's, and you and Simon wished you could be adopted so that you could be "special", too!' She sighed ruefully. 'I think it's mainly due to Mum and Dad's sensible loving that we've turned out as level-headed as we have.'

Sonia hugged her again before stepping back. 'You're going to be just as sensible with your baby, you'll see.' She began to tidy up. 'And Justin is such a nice man, he deserves to be happy this time.' She ran the steaming hot water into the sink, putting in the plates to soak.

It took a few seconds for what she had said to sink in, but once it did Caroline stared at her back with puzzled eyes. This time?

She swallowed hard. 'I'm glad you and Tony like him so much,' she answered dazedly. *This time?*

Sonia turned to give her a brief smile. 'Once you get past the surface coldness you can't help but like him. And I suppose it's only natural that he should have built up defences after what happened,' she chattered on.

'Yes,' she agreed hollowly. *After what happened?* She had completely lost her grip on this conversation, had no idea what Sonia was talking about.

'I know how unhappy I would be if anything happened to Tony and me.' Sonia shook her head. 'And she could only have been young,' she added sadly. 'It seems such a waste.'

The evening had been too long, been too fraught with tension already; Caroline swayed tiredly as she tried to make sense of the conversation. It had something to do with Justin's past, of that she was certain, but the little he had told her himself, about his childhood, his parents' death, didn't include any 'she'. Except the Penny he spoke of in his dreams. Could this puzzling conversation have anything to do with her?

'It must have been a terrible time for Justin,' Sonia continued, completely unaware that Caroline had no idea what she was talking about as she did the dishes without looking round.

'Yes,' Caroline agreed again, desperate to know what she had so far been afraid to ask Justin, fearing the end of their marriage if she did.

'But now he has you.' Sonia turned to smile at her. 'He has a whole new life with you and the baby you're expecting. He already seems so much more—relaxed than he did when the two of you were first married.' She resumed washing the dishes. 'I hope you didn't mind Tony telling me about the death of Justin's first wife.' She frowned. 'It's such a private thing, really, but Paula told Tony, and so Tony told me . . . I just——'

Caroline was no longer listening to her sister's chatter. *Justin had been married before!*

CHAPTER EIGHT

CAROLINE hadn't wanted to look at it, hadn't wanted to see the indisputable proof which told her that not only had Justin lied to her about believing in love, he had also not told her of his first wife, a woman he *had* loved.

She hadn't seen their marriage certificate since Justin had slipped it into his pocket after their wedding, but there under the marital status column for Justin was the word 'widower'!

Caroline didn't know how long she had been staring at it, feeling completely numb. Widowers were elderly gentlemen, men who had lived a lifetime with the woman they loved, not men of Justin's age who hadn't had a life at all! She couldn't think how she had missed this tangible evidence on their wedding day, except that she had been so ecstatically happy that day she hadn't really seen anything at all except Justin.

She had somehow managed to get through the last of the previous evening, agreeing eagerly when Justin suggested they leave shortly after she and Sonia returned from the kitchen. And if Justin had noticed that she was a little quieter than usual he had obviously put it down to a reaction to Paula's bitchiness, also seeming to understand when she had been the one to suggest she was too tired for lovemaking.

She had barely slept, still too numb from what Sonia had unwittingly revealed to her, too stunned to confront Justin for the truth just then. But this morning, after he had left for work, she had found their marriage certificate locked away in Justin's desk along with his other private papers—although a heartbreaking search had revealed no previous marriage certificate for Justin. To Penny.

Penny had to have been Justin's first wife; it was too obvious not to be the truth. And if, as Caroline suspected, Penny was also the reason Justin had had a vasectomy, preferring not to have any children at all if they couldn't be the children of the woman he had loved, then it would mean the end of *their* marriage. While she had still held out hope that Justin would eventually come to love their child, she had been willing to try anything to keep their marriage intact, but she wouldn't —couldn't—subject her child to a lifetime of rejection by its father because it wasn't the child of the woman he had loved. That would be a cruelty to them all.

She felt for Justin, knew he must have suffered terribly after his first wife's death, even sympathised with his decision not to allow love into his life again. But there had been so many things he had never told her about himself that she was beginning to wonder if they had ever really had a marriage. Marriage had to be more than pleasing each other in bed! Where was the sharing, the confiding, the *trusting?*

She felt betrayed, deeply let down, was hurting so badly she wanted to cry and never stop. But the tears wouldn't come, and neither would the release from the numbing pain. Only Justin could help her now, and she doubted that he would want to, not in the way she needed to be helped. For that he would have to tell her he no longer loved Penny; and she knew that wasn't true. He would have to tell her he wanted the child she carried; and she knew that wasn't true either.

The dream that had begun so fragilely now seemed set to shatter into irretrievable pieces.

It wasn't the ideal time for Don Lindford to pay his return call, but when Mrs Avery came into the living-room later that day to tell her he was outside in the hallway she knew she would have to see him, if only to tell him how sorry Justin was to have missed him the last time he called.

'Mr Lindford.' She rose smilingly to greet him, doing her best to put aside her despair at least for the duration of his visit.

'Don,' he gently reproved, taking the hand she held out to him.

He was just as charmingly handsome as ever, slightly more tanned than he had been the last time she had seen him, but then Justin had said he had been out of the country. After the typically British summer they had just had he would have had to have been to have acquired a tan at all.

'Don,' she returned. 'Won't you sit down?' she

invited politely, sitting in the chair opposite his as he did so. 'I'm afraid Justin isn't here again,' she explained apologetically.

'So I understand.' He nodded slowly.

'He will be in his office all of this afternoon though, if you would like to——'

'I can't, I'm afraid,' he said regretfully, his brown eyes warm, his sandy-coloured hair slightly ruffled from the breeze outside. 'I just called in on the off-chance on my way to the airport.'

'You're going away again?' Her eyes widened. She didn't know why she had, but she had presumed Don Lindford was a lawyer like Justin; if he were he had some very strange clients to need to go out of the country so much. 'Justin tried to contact you after your last visit,' she explained at his questioning look, 'but apparently you were out of the country then, too.'

He smiled. 'Didn't Justin tell you I'm in the import/export business?'

'No.' That explained so much!

'It can sometimes make me—elusive,' he added enigmatically.

'That's what Justin said,' she acknowledged ruefully.

'Did he?' Don chuckled. 'He knows me so well.'

'It would seem so.' She returned his smile ruefully. 'I gather the two of you have been friends for a long time.'

'And I gather,' he said teasingly, 'that the "pack" is about to increase by one. It is just one, isn't it?' he prompted mischievously.

Because she was so naturally slender her pregnancy had begun to show almost immediately, and now at four months she had a definite 'bump' to clearly reveal her condition.

'As far as we know,' she said drily.

'Your brother and sister are twins, aren't they?'

Her eyes widened. 'How did you know that?' she asked curiously.

He frowned, shrugging. 'Someone must have mentioned it,' he dismissed. 'Justin's unexpected marriage to you caused quite a lot of gossip at the time, you know,' he added teasingly.

'I can imagine,' she acknowledged disgustedly; how much more speculation it would cause if their marriage came to an abrupt end! 'I can't bear gossip,' she snapped impatiently.

'Most of it was from jealous women who would have given anything to be in your place,' Don pointed out.

Like Paula. 'I can understand that,' she accepted heavily. 'Can I offer you a drink this time, Don?' She gave a wan smile.

'Afraid not,' he answered ruefully. 'I really am, literally, on my way to the airport. But I'll take a raincheck, though, for the next time I come to see Justin.'

'Perhaps he'll even be here next time.' She sighed. 'The weekend is really the best time to find him at home,' she advised.

'Right.' He stood up. 'It's been nice meeting you again, Caroline.'

'And you.' She walked out to the door with him.

'You must come to dinner when you return from your trip abroad.'

His grin widened. 'As soon as Justin feels up to sharing the company of his wife!'

Her smile didn't quite reach her eyes. 'He's looking forward to seeing you again, I can assure you.'

'We'll see,' Don said non-committally.

'Where are you off to?' Caroline enquired politely.

'A few days here, a few days there.' He shrugged dismissively. 'In my business you're never quite sure where you're going to be tomorrow.'

'Obviously.' She gave a rueful smile. 'Well, I wish you success on this latest business trip.'

'Thanks.' His gaze was warm. 'And you take care of your wolf and cub, OK?'

'OK.' She laughed softly.

His fist lightly grazed her jaw. 'Justin is a very lucky man,' he murmured admiringly.

Her eyes were suddenly shadowed. 'I'll tell him you said that.'

Don straightened, looking at his narrow gold wrist-watch. 'You do that,' he nodded absently. 'I have to dash if I don't want to miss my plane,' he said regretfully.

Caroline turned slowly away from the closed door once he had left; she would make sure she didn't forget to tell Justin about his visit this time! It was unfortunate that they kept missing each other.

She couldn't help wondering if part of Don's initial surprise at finding Justin had married her was because he had known Penny, known how much Justin loved the other woman.

'Has Mr Lindford gone?'

She drew in a deep breath before raising her head to look at Mrs Avery, frowning deeply as she saw how worried the other woman looked. 'What is it, Mrs Avery?' she asked, voicing her own concern at how pale the elderly woman looked. 'What's wrong?'

'I'm not really sure.' The housekeeper shook her head. 'Mr de Wolfe told me that if ever Mr Lindford called again I was to telephone him straight away and let him know. But——'

'What on earth for?' Caroline was puzzled now: did Justin want to see the other man so much, and was he afraid she would once again forget to tell him of his visit?

'I don't know,' the older woman returned, 'but I did just as he asked, and now Mr Lindford's left before Mr de Wolfe returned, and——'

'Justin is coming home?' Caroline was even more puzzled.

'Yes. But I——' The housekeeper broke off as she heard a key put in the lock.

Caroline stared at Justin in some surprise, although she had known it had to be him; she had never seen him quite so distraught before, his hair looking as if he had run his fingers through it many times, his face pale beneath naturally dark skin.

She also knew he must have driven as if the devil were at his heels to get home in the short time since Mrs Avery must have called him. What on earth had made him so upset about Don Lindford's visit that he had risked having an accident in this way?

'Where is he?' His voice was grim.

'Justin——'

'Where is he, Caroline?' He prompted in a fiercely hushed voice.

'He's gone. But——'

'Damn!' Justin slammed his clenched fist against his thigh. 'Damn him!' He closed his eyes in frustrated anger.

'Justin.' She shot a pointed glance in Mrs Avery's direction, the poor woman looking more bewildered than ever. As she was. But she wasn't about to satisfy her curiosity out here in the hallway; she and Justin had too much to discuss for that.

He relaxed only slightly, attempting to give the housekeeper a reassuring smile. 'Thank you for calling me so promptly,' he told her gently. 'Could Mrs de Wolfe and I have some tea in the lounge now, please?'

Mrs Avery seemed glad of something to do and hurried off to her kitchen, where her pots and pans didn't cause her half so much worry as the two humans she worked for.

Caroline turned back to Justin. 'Perhaps now you wouldn't mind telling me what all that was about?' she said irritably, disturbed by the way Justin had burst in here asking for the other man.

He sighed. 'Let's go through to the lounge,' he suggested firmly.

She preceded him into the room in tight-lipped

frustration, even though she realised they couldn't carry out their conversation in the hallway.

'Really, Justin,' she turned to him impatiently as soon as they were in the privacy of the lounge, 'why on earth did you rush home in that way just to see Don Lindford? Or was it just to see him? She frowned suddenly. 'You didn't think I was attracted to him, did you?' She was horrified at the thought.

'Of course not,' Justin grated abruptly. 'Damn it, Caroline, I—what did he want?' he demanded, his gaze narrowed.

'To see you again, of course.' She moved restlessly about the room.

'Caroline.' He spoke slowly, worriedly. 'Hasn't it ever occurred to you that Lindford calls at very strange times if he expects to find me at home?'

She ceased her pacing, looking at him questioningly. 'Well, yes, of course it has,' she confirmed hesitantly. 'But last time he just called on the off-chance, and this time he said he was on his way to the airport and thought he would just drop in——'

'The airport?' Justin echoed sharply. 'He's going out of the country again?'

She nodded. 'So he said. He said he's in the import/export business, so I——'

'Did he indeed?' Justin snorted derisively. 'I doubt very much——' He had come to an abrupt halt next to the tiny table that stood beside the chair Caroline had been sitting in earlier, and slowly picked up the folded piece of paper there. He shot Caroline a puzzled look as he held their marriage certificate in his artistically slender hands.

Caroline stiffened. She had left the certificate out, intending to talk to Justin about his previous marriage, only they had become side-tracked by the subject of Don Lindford. Now she felt like a child caught with her hand in the cookie jar. Which was ridiculous. It was their marriage certificate, for goodness' sake! And she wasn't the one who had been keeping secrets . . .

'There's no need to look at me like that,' she snapped defensively, her nerves strung out to breaking point. 'It's *our* marriage certificate.'

'Yes?' he prompted calmly—too calmly!

'I wanted to see it!'

'Obviously.' Justin nodded, his gaze narrowed on her in slow speculation.

Caroline sighed. 'I think you can guess why,' she bit out impatiently, hating being made to feel on the defensive like this, feeling very much as she had at their first meeting when she had felt at such a disadvantage by his blunt honesty.

'Guess why you went into my desk, looked through the papers there?' he queried pleasantly. 'Actually, no,' he said harshly. 'I can't imagine why you would feel this sudden urge to see our marriage certificate. Perhaps you doubted its legality?' he derided harshly. 'Or maybe you were just hoping there had been some sort of mistake?'

'Why on earth would I hope a thing like that?' she gasped in a pained voice.

He shrugged broad shoulders. 'Things have always been strained between us,' he grated.

'Maybe you realise this marriage wasn't such a good idea after all.'

Her eyes widened. 'Is that the way you feel about it?'

'We weren't discussing me,' Justin said abruptly.

She gave a ragged sigh. 'Of course I don't want to end our marriage,' she dismissed impatiently. 'I just—— I wanted to see our marriage certificate. I—something Sonia said last night made it—necessary,' she finished awkwardly.

He stiffened warily, suddenly tense. 'Something *Sonia* said?' he repeated softly.

Caroline swallowed hard, her heart fluttering nervously now that she could no longer put off discussing the fact that he had been married before. 'She mentioned your first marriage,' she told Justin in a rush, colour burning her cheeks at the same time that his seemed to pale. 'Quite—casually, innocently.' She shrugged awkwardly. 'She thought I already knew, you see,' she added emotionally, wishing she could remain calmly in control, but the subject was still too new to her for her to cope with it in the way she had all the other surprises her marriage had revealed.

Justin gave a weary sigh, the marriage certificate fluttering back down on to the table as he moved his hand to run his fingers distractedly through his hair. 'Yes—I do see,' he finally answered in a raggedly disjointed voice. 'The marriage certificate confirms that I was married before,' he conceded flatly.

'Yes,' she nodded, her eyes pained.

'And now you want to know about——'

'Penny,' she put in firmly.

He frowned darkly. 'How do you know her name?' he demanded suspiciously.

'Dreams. *Your* dreams,' she revealed. 'When you called out for her.' She deliberately kept her voice devoid of emotion, not wanting it to sound like an accusation, even though his calling for the other woman had made her feel betrayed.

'Oh, God.' He groaned, his gaze momentarily hidden from her as he squeezed his eyes tightly shut. The memories were all there in the silver-grey depth once he looked at her again. 'I'm sorry for that,' he told her heavily. 'I thought they had all stopped. I—I am sorry you had to find out about Penny that way.'

Caroline moistened her lips. 'All I learnt from your dreams was that you had a woman in your life called Penny. I didn't realise until last night that she had been your wife.'

His gaze widened. 'Then what——' He broke off abruptly as Mrs Avery bustled in with the tray of tea.

'Sorry I took so long.' She seemed unaware of the tension in the room, her flushed cheeks telling of her own flustered mood. 'The telephone rang. And then I realised I had forgotten to put the kettle on. And then—but you don't want to hear all this.' She suddenly seemed to realise that the silence in the room was fraught with an expectant tension. 'I'll go and see about dinner,' she awkwardly excused herself.

'Poor Mrs Avery.' Caroline gave the ghost of a smile as the tiny woman hurried from the room. 'She isn't used to all this.'

'I don't think any of us are,' Justin bit out, seeming more in control after the brief interruption. 'If you didn't know Penny had been my wife, what *did* you think she was?' He watched her closely.

Caroline drew in a ragged breath. 'I believed that—that she was the woman you loved. I didn't know she was dead.'

'If I loved another woman, why did I marry you?' he demanded impatiently.

'Any number or reasons.' She shrugged ruefully. 'Penny could have been married to someone else. Or maybe she couldn't accept your decision about not having children. Or perhaps——'

'I get the general idea,' Justin bit out raspingly. 'When did these—dreams start?' he frowned darkly.

She sighed. 'The night we first went to dinner with Sonia and Tony. The first night you hadn't—hadn't——' She couldn't put into words the start of her disillusionment when he had rejected her so cruelly.

'Oh, my God,' he groaned emotionally. 'And when I called out for Penny later that night you thought it was because I loved her!' He grasped Caroline's arms painfully, forcing her to look at him. 'Darling, it wasn't that at all——'

'Don't call me that.' She wrenched away from him, her eyes dark with pain. 'You loved her. I could tell that you loved her!'

'Of course I did,' he admitted dismissively. 'But it was twelve years ago, Caroline. I'm not even the same person now that I was then!'

'I know that,' she choked. 'The man you are today is incapable of feeling love!'

The hands he had been raising to grasp hers suddenly clenched into fists instead, Justin recoiling as if he had been struck.

He turned away from her, his breathing ragged. 'Can't you see,' he finally bit out forcefully, 'how much loving someone hurts?'

'I know exactly how much it hurts,' she choked, her love for him clearly revealed in her pain-filled eyes if he would only care to turn and look at her.

And he did turn, flinching back from her as if she had dealt him a physical blow. 'I never asked for your love.' He shook his head, coldness in his gaze now. 'I told you from the first how I felt about it.'

'But you didn't reject my love when I first offered it to you!' she reminded him raggedly.

'No,' he conceded heavily. 'I'd hoped—wanted——' He breathed harshly. 'Where do we go from here?'

Caroline felt as if part of her had curled up inside her and died. What had she expected, that Justin would suddenly get down on his knees and declare his undying love for her, tell her that no matter how he had felt in the past he could no longer deny his love for her and their child? Those were the things that dreams were made of, and when a man was as determined as Justin never to fall in love again they were destined to remain just that, dreams.

'*You* don't go anywhere,' she sighed shakily. 'But I have to go. You must see that.'

No emotion showed on his face; she might just as well have told him she intended going out shopping, not that she was leaving him and not coming back!

'Like all women, I had foolish dreams,' she dismissed self-derisively, her heart breaking inside. 'But now I think it would be best, for all of us——' she had to think of her child, and the man standing before her could never love anyone '—if I just left.' She held her head up proudly in defiance of the pain that threatened to rip her apart.

Justin still stood unmoving—and unmoved. 'I can't let you do that,' he murmured softly.

As if any of them had a choice any more! She had to believe they would all be better off her way, she because she would no longer be constantly seeking the unattainable, her baby because it would grow up knowing only love, and Justin because he was happiest when he wasn't forced to acknowledge emotion. It didn't matter that she would always love him, not when she had her child to consider, too.

She gave a dismissive shake of her head. 'I wasn't asking your permission, Justin,' she stated huskily. 'This is the way it has to be.'

'No.'

'Justin——'

'Not yet, Caroline,' he insisted harshly. 'If you still want to go in a few months' time then I'll help you set up your new home. I'm sure Mrs Avery will be only too pleased to accompany you wherever you want to go,' he added drily. 'Her loyalties had changed by about the second day you moved in,' he conceded ruefully.

'I'll be pleased to have her,' Caroline accepted distractedly, 'but I'm most certainly not waiting a few months before I leave.'

'I can't let you go just yet.' Justin shook his head.

'And I already told you I don't need your permission!' She was becoming deeply agitated; why couldn't he at least let her leave with her dignity intact! 'Justin, don't let's prolong this. Let's just end things while we're at least still friends.'

He gave a tight, humourless smile. 'I'm not asking this to hurt you any more. I just—Caroline, why don't you sit down? You've been under enough strain for one day.' He frowned. 'All this can't be good for the baby.'

'Please don't pretend that it matters to you,' she said sadly. 'That would be too cruel.'

'I certainly don't want you to lose it, and if I——' He broke off, breathing harshly. 'You have to stay here!'

Caroline looked at him searchingly. 'Why?' she finaly prompted huskily.

'Is your pregnancy going well?' he probed anxiously. 'Is the doctor satisfied that everything is—normal?'

'Very normal,' she confirmed warily. 'Justin, tell me what's wrong?' she urged with a sudden certainty that something definitely was wrong!

He drew in a deep breath. 'You once asked me about—well, about this.' He put a hand up to his velvet-covered eye.

'Yes?' She felt a strange churning in her chest.

Justin nodded abruptly, seeming to be searching for the right words. 'There is no easy way to tell you this,' he finally bit out harshly. 'You're sure nothing is—going to happen, to you or the baby?' He looked at her anxiously.

'I can't promise.' She shook her head. 'But if it's something that I have a right to know, something that affects my leaving today, then I think you should tell me.'

'At least sit down,' he encouraged softly.

She couldn't see how having her sit down was going to make any difference if what he were about to tell her was so disturbing, but she did as he requested anyway, sensing that he really was anxious nothing should happen to the baby.

'The tea is probably cold by now, but——'

'Justin, I don't want any tea,' Caroline told him patiently. 'I just want to know what's bothering you.'

'Lindford is what's bothering me!' he bit out forcefully.

'Don Lindford?' she repeated in a bewildered voice. 'But what does he have to do——' She broke off, paling as she remembered what Justin had said a few minutes ago. 'You mean he——' She swallowed hard, nausea quickly rising. 'He's the one——'

'——who blinded me,' Justin finished grimly, his fingers moving absently against the black velvet that covered the unseeing orb. 'Yes, he's the one,' he confirmed harshly. 'And until I find out what he intends to take from me this time, I can't let you leave here!'

CHAPTER NINE

CAROLINE looked up at him with bewildered eyes. 'Take from you?' she repeated dazedly.

Justin came down on his haunches beside her chair, taking her chilled hands in his. 'Surely you can see that he's been coming here for a reason, that his friendly little promises to "see me again soon" are no more than veiled threats?' he explained grimly.

Yes, she could see that now, now that she knew the other man had deliberately injured Justin in the past because of the wrong he considered he had done him.

She would never have guessed that the pleasantly attractive man was responsible for blinding Justin, his ready charm having lulled her into a false sense of security where he was concerned. It gave her a shiver down her spine to recall how friendly he had seemed, how he had talked to her teasingly as if he were an old friend of Justin's who had just heard of his marriage. She didn't need to be told where he had been 'away' so that he was unable to attend their wedding as he had claimed. It would have been a little difficult for him to have got out of prison for the day!

God, how he must laughed at her for her

159

ignorance about him. And Justin was right about those veiled threats; she recognised them for exactly what they were now. She also realised what Justin had already known, that the other man's visits while he was at work hadn't been accidental at all, that Don Lindford had been well aware of the fact that Justin wouldn't be at home at that time of the day.

Last time he had taken the sight of one of Justin's eyes as his retribution; what did he intend to take this time?

'Oh, God, Justin!' She paled even more as realisation hit her. 'He knows about the baby.' She clutched at him frantically. 'He realised this afternoon that I was pregnant, and congratulated me on the fact.' Her eyes were wild. 'He wouldn't try to—try to—— God! Justin,' she choked again. 'The man's dangerous, his vindictiveness is a sickness. Can't you do anything to stop him?' She gazed up at him anxiously.

'The police already know of his last visit——'

'They do?' she pounced eagerly.

He nodded slowly, his gaze gently apologetic. 'I was afraid to tell you before who he was in case anything happened to the baby. I didn't want to risk causing you to miscarry,' he told her grimly. 'But I had to stop you leaving me, and leaving yourself open to Lindford's schemes.' He looked at her searchingly. 'Maybe I should call your doctor now and get him to check you over. This must have been a shock to you, and——'

'Justin, babies, and pregnant women, are much

stronger than you realise,' she sighed. 'I don't even feel a twinge of discomfort. And no doctor would thank you for bringing him here for no reason other than your own worry.'

'I don't give a damn whether he would thank me or not,' he rasped. *'You're* what's important.'

She could see that she was important to him, that although Justin still didn't want their child—*his* child—he couldn't bear to see anything happen to her or it. She didn't know which it was worse to feel, the futile love she had for Justin, or his own inability to recognise love, to acknowledge it even if he did recognise it.

'You should have told me about Don Lindford, Justin,' she frowned. 'It's been weeks since his last visit.' She gave an involuntary shiver as she realised he had been as close to her in this room as Justin was now.

'I've alerted the police, although there isn't anything they can do unless he actually commits a crime, except warn him to behave himself, and they've already done that.' He grimaced. 'Paying a visit and congratulating you on your pregnancy can't be considered a threat. But Mrs Avery knew to call me if he came here again.'

'You've been treating me like a child who had to be protected from the truth, Justin——'

'It was *your* child I was concerned about. Can't you see that?' he interrupted angrily. 'I knew you would never forgive me if anything happened to the baby because of who and what I am,' he said bitterly. 'You've forgiven me a lot of things, but even you wouldn't have been able to accept that!'

'You still should have told me, shouldn't have kept this to yourself.' Her eyes suddenly widened as she realised Don Lindford knew all about her family too, and now that she knew who he was, and what he had done to Justin in the past, she very much doubted that he had acquired that knowledge through gossip about her and Justin, as he had claimed he had. He seemed to have an obsessive need to know all about Justin, and the people who were close to him. 'My family have to be warned——'

'Tony already knows to take care of Sonia, and your parents are sensible people, too. Unfortunately, paying me social calls can't be considered a crime,' Justin grated, his gaze bleak.

'But he didn't come to see you. I'm sure seeing me here alone was deliber—— What do you mean, Tony already knows about it?' She looked puzzled as she realised what he had said. 'You told him?' she frowned.

Justin gave an abrupt nod of his head. 'The night we first went over there for dinner. You had mentioned Lindford's visit, and Tony saw my reaction to it. He realised something wasn't quite right about Lindford's visit. In the circumstances I thought it best that he know.' He shrugged.

'So that's why he seemed different when the two of you got back from buying the champagne,' Caroline said slowly.

'Yes,' Justin sighed. 'As soon as we were out of the door he started asking questions.' He looked at her ruefully. 'Once he knew the truth about Lindford he agreed with me about not telling you yet, something to do with the early months of pregnancy being the most delicate. As it turned out it was the best thing; it saved you six weeks of unnecessary worry. When anything might have happened,' he added pointedly.

For someone who proclaimed to care nothing for their child he had been very anxious that no harm should come to it! Unless that really was because he believed she would blame him if she miscarried because of a past he could do nothing about. She suddenly felt too tired to battle with her own thoughts any more today, feeling weak and ill.

She sighed wearily. 'It seems I have no choice but to stay here until we find out what—game this man Lindford is playing with us.' Worry etched her brow. 'I wish—oh!' She gave a start of surprise as she clutched instinctively at the slight swelling that was the baby.

Justin was instantly at her side, his face very pale, his gaze darkly shadowed. 'What is it?' he demanded anxiously. 'Is it the baby? Oh, my God,' he choked. 'I didn't——'

'It is the baby, Justin.' She spoke calmly, soothingly, her expression serene. 'But nothing is wrong. I just felt a fluttering movement, like the gentle beat of a butterfly's wing.' Tears of happiness glistened in her eyes as she looked up at him emotionally. 'I felt our son or daughter move inside me for the first time!' she told him shakily.

He seemed to pale even more, shaking his head

as he moved away from her. 'You couldn't have done,' he gasped. 'It's too soon, surely?'

'About sixteen weeks the doctor told me it can occasionally be felt, and I'm just over that, although it is usually about twenty weeks.' She gazed up at him yearningly. 'It's the strangest sensation, and yet the most beautiful too. I——'

'I think you should go and lie down,' he cut in abruptly, keeping his gaze averted from where her hands still rested lightly against their baby. 'I'll have Mrs Avery prepare an early dinner and then I think you should get some rest. And you don't need to worry, I'll be sleeping in the guest-room from now on!'

Caroline watched in dismay as he strode briskly from the room. Nothing was going to change, it never would change; she had been a fool to hope that it ever would. She could only hope she wasn't forced to stay here too much longer.

But their lives did change irrevocably after that day, with not even the physical closeness there now to prevent Justin and herself from becoming complete strangers.

They went about their lives separately, often not seeing each other for days at a time, Justin often eating dinner in his study while Caroline had a tray in her room. If Mrs Avery was aware of the estrangement she wisely said nothing.

They heard nothing from Don Lindford in the weeks that followed, and it seemed that he was still out of the country. Justin had his own ideas as to the purpose of these 'business trips' but proving it would be difficult, although it almost seemed as if the other man was daring Justin to try and prove anything against him by telling him of his 'import/export' business.

Neither of them had any doubt that he meant to keep to his promise to see Justin again!

Caroline was dismayed when she realised that she and Justin never had finished their conversation about his first wife, about how and why the other woman had died. Not that it really mattered, Caroline acknowledged, not when Justin's ability to love had died with her. She didn't need to know anything more about his first marriage than that.

Despite the worry about Don Lindford, and the state of her marriage, the pregnancy was going well. The baby moved all the time now, seemed extremely active. It was an experience she should have been able to share with Justin, but after the last time she had attempted it she didn't dare. As a result, the baby was growing nicely and *she* was losing weight. By the end of her fifth month she felt too dispirited to continue working. She was sad to let her career go and to say goodbye to all the wonderful people she had come to know at the hospital, but really felt she wasn't doing her patients or herself any good by continuing. But the extra time at the apartment that no longer seemed like home to her didn't bring her any comfort.

After two weeks of wandering about the perfectly neat and tidy rooms, when she was even beginning to get on Mrs Avery's nerves with her constant listlessness, Caroline knew she couldn't stand living like this any longer, that it was time for her to start getting on with the rest of her life.

'No!' Justin bit out furiously that evening when she told him she was going to start looking around for somewhere else to live.

She sighed brokenly at his implacability. 'I can't live like this any more!'

His mouth tightened as his gaze flickered over her finely etched features and too-slender body. 'And what about Lindford?'

She made an impatient movement. 'If he's that dangerous why don't the police arrest him?' She knew she was behaving unreasonably, but she just couldn't cope any more.

'There's a little matter of evidence, Caroline,' Justin reminded her in a rasping voice. 'He hasn't committed any crime—that they're yet aware of,' he added grimly.

If the last weeks had been hard on her, Justin hadn't fared any better, his face thinner, lines of tiredness beside his eyes, no sign any more of even his arrogant humour. They were making each other more unhappy than was necessary by this enforced continuation of their sham of a marriage. Anyone looking at them could see they were unhappy together.

'He could go on like this for years,' she pointed out restlessly.

'He won't,' Justin said with certainty. 'Sooner or later he's going to get tired of playing.'

'And if it's later?' She sighed her frustration with the situation, not even caring at that moment that, when Don Lindford did tire of playing, someone might get hurt. She was too tired and angry to think rationally.

Justin shrugged. 'I can't see that it's going to harm you to continue living with me like this,' he bit out, his eyes narrowed. 'What's really changed, Caroline?' he derided. 'Only that we no longer share a bed!'

She flinched. 'You're right.' She was suddenly very still. 'We always were strangers anywhere else but there.'

He frowned darkly. 'I didn't mean it like— Caroline!' he called after her as she fled the room.

He made no effort to follow her to the bedroom she now slept in alone, and for that she felt grateful. These damned tears, she cursed the flood that cascaded down her cheeks; the morning sickness had passed only to be replaced by tears that fell at the slightest provocation. And living with Justin the way that she was at the moment there was all too much of that! She cried because she was bored and restless, she cried because there seemed too much to do, she cried because she loved Justin, she cried because she hated him a little, too. Anything could make her cry, even the fact that it was raining outside.

Justin was right, she couldn't leave here just yet. And that made her cry, too!

The socialising they had to do made matters even

worse. Her whole family seemed to like Justin, and when they dined with her parents Simon usually managed to be there now, his admiration for Justin so great that he was contemplating becoming a lawyer, too, once he had left university. Even being with Sonia and Tony was a strain, although Tony, at least, was aware of the situation concerning Don Lindford.

The situation also seemed to have brought out Tony's protective instincts where Sonia was concerned, to have shown him his true feelings for his wife, his love for her now undoubted. And if nothing else good had come out of the mess, Caroline could at least be glad that had. Tony and Sonia's marriage was going to last; she was sure of it.

Although she wasn't quite so certain of that when Sonia turned up at the apartment swearing and cursing about her husband.

'How dare he!' She marched into the apartment after Caroline, having nothing else to do, had opened the door to her ring. 'Treating me as if I'm six years old, like I have no sense at all—yes, just as if all I have between my ears is fresh air!' She glared across the width of the lounge at Caroline, who watched her rather bemusedly. 'And you're no better,' she suddenly accused, her blue eyes blazing furiously. 'I realise I'm your "baby sister", but how could you keep something like this from me? I thought we were close, closer than ever before after admitting how guilty we felt about our jealousy of each other as children. And now you——'

'Sonia, would you calm down and tell me what's wrong?' she prompted ruefully. 'Let me ask Mrs Avery to get us some tea,' she said persuasively. 'And then——'

'Tea!' her sister echoed explosively. 'I don't want any tea, I just want an explanation!'

She held up her hands in a defensive shrug. 'For what?' Caroline was completely puzzled by her sister's outburst. 'Darling, you aren't still imagining that Tony is in love with me, are you? Because——'

'Of course not,' Sonia dismissed impatiently. 'Although at the time I wasn't imagining it,' she added firmly. 'What I am talking about is the fact that no one troubled to tell me about this man Lindford!' She glared.

'Oh.' Caroline turned away with a sigh. 'That,' she grimaced.

'*That?*' Sonia exploded. 'Some man has been going around threatening you, issuing obscure threats to all of us, and all you can say is "Oh—that"!'

Caroline sighed. 'I gather Tony told you about him?'

Her sister nodded impatiently. 'He's been like an old mother hen lately, wanting to know where I am all the time, when I'll be home, things like that. At first I was quite flattered that he seemed to be acting jealously,' she admitted ruefully. 'Then I began to feel as if he didn't trust me for some reason, and I didn't like that.'

She could see by Sonia's mutinous expression that she hadn't. 'The poor man told you out of self-defence!' she realised with a shake of her head.

'So what if he did?' her sister said unrepentantly. 'He should have told me what was going on weeks ago.'

Caroline sighed. 'I only found out myself a short time ago.'

'But you didn't say a word about it to me,' Sonia rebuked her. 'He could have—could have——You shouldn't have kept it to yourself, Caroline.'

'Justin and Tony ganged up on us,' she said ruefully. 'But they only did what they thought was best, although I have to admit I was as angry as you to start with,' she reasoned as her sister seemed about to protest again. 'Look at it from their point of view,' she pointed out gently. 'They didn't want to worry either of us.' The last thing any of them needed was Sonia becoming so angry about the situation that she continued her argument with Tony!

'Of course not,' Sonia agreed slowly, looking ruefully at Caroline's obvious pregnancy. 'I'm sorry, love, for coming here and going on like this, but I was just so angry at being treated like a child——'

'So was I.' She smiled.

'Gave Justin hell, hm?' As Caroline had intended, Sonia began to relax, the fire dying out of her eyes as she sank down into one of the armchairs.

'Do you think that's possible?' Caroline sat

down, too, now that the danger had passed; Sonia could be totally unreasonable if she allowed herself to stay angry.

'I think it's possible for you to do anything where Justin is concerned.' Sonia wrinkled her nose prettily. 'He's obviously very much in love with you.'

She remained outwardly calm, but inside she was dying a little more. She didn't know how Justin felt about anything any more, but even if he did love her she knew that even to keep her with him he wouldn't ever tell her of that love. And even if he could admit to feeling something for her, there was still the baby to consider, the child he didn't want.

'I was—a little angry with him at the time,' she admitted dismissively.

'Like I was a "little angry" with Tony,' Sonia said teasingly.

Her mouth quirked in amusement. 'Probably.'

'Men!' Sonia shook her head. 'When will they learn that women aren't made of delicate china?'

'I can't say I altogether mind being protected,' Caroline said thoughtfully, remembering the warm glow she always felt in Justin's arms. 'Even if that is disloyal to the liberated female.'

'It is, but I'm afraid I feel the same way,' her sister confided. 'Although don't, for goodness' sake, tell Tony that!'

Caroline laughed softly. 'I won't. Would you like that tea now?'

'Why not?' Sonia accepted lightly. 'In view of the fact that you shouldn't drink anything stronger

I think it will do as a celebration drink.'

She rang for Mrs Avery. 'What are we celebrating?' She frowned her puzzlement, briefly
breaking off the conversation to ask for the tray of
tea before turning curiously back to Sonia.

'Why the fact that it's all over, of course,' her
sister commented with impatient indulgence for her
puzzlement.

Caroline became suddenly still, her heart beating
faster, her mouth dry. 'Do you really think it is?'
she said enigmatically.

'Of course.' Sonia scorned her lack of confidence. 'The American authorities have this man
Lindford now; they've charged him with everything from illegal parking to arms smuggling.
Justin says he's in real trouble.'

She swallowed hard. 'Tony told you that, too?'

'I'd have killed him if he hadn't,' her sister told
her lightly. 'Justin told him the good news a couple
of days ago; it was because Tony suddenly *stopped*
asking me where I was going that I became sus-
picious!' she added ruefully. 'Personally I hope
they put him away for a long time——'

Caroline was no longer listening. Justin had
known for at least two days that Don Lindford no
longer posed a threat to any of them, and *he hadn't
told her!*

CHAPTER TEN

WHEN Caroline had asked Justin about Don Lindford on the few occasions they had talked together he had told her the other man was still proving elusive. If Sonia were to be believed, and Caroline had no reason to believe Tony would lie to her sister—every reason to be sure he hadn't now that he was familiar with her sister's temper!—then that was no longer true.

Why hadn't Justin told her that?

The only answer that seemed possible was that he hadn't wanted her to leave. But that didn't sound like the Justin she knew, the Justin who had assured her that once this was over he would help her find somewhere else to live, that he was only keeping her here for her own safety.

He was late home that evening but Caroline was waiting in the living-room for him, having assured Mrs Avery that she could see to serving dinner for the two of them tonight. If they wanted any. Personally she didn't think she could eat a thing.

'Justin?' she called to him before he could disappear into his study for the rest of the evening.

He was frowning heavily when he appeared in the doorway, tall and dark, the eye-patch giving him the appearance of a misplaced pirate. 'Yes?' he prompted abruptly, his manner not forthcoming.

He was more a stranger to her now that he had ever been, but she still loved him more than he seemed to believe it was possible to love anyone. Her hands rested self-consciously on the rounded swell of her body, the same swell that prevented her putting her hands anywhere else. 'I want —need—to talk to you,' she told him huskily.

His brows rose. 'Can't it wait until I've had a shower and changed?'

'No,' she said flatly.

Justin put down his briefcase in one of the armchairs with forceful movements, striding into the room to look down at her, his gaze hooded. 'You didn't see the doctor today, did you?' he frowned. 'I thought that wasn't until next week.'

The fact that he was aware of her routine check-ups with her doctor at all came as something of a surprise to her; that he knew when they were stunned her.

His mouth tightened as he saw her reaction to his question. 'Mrs Avery chatters on about them as if I should be interested in every twinge!' he bit out dismissively.

Dull acceptance darkened her eyes to the colour of sapphires. For a moment she had actually believed he had taken an interest in her pregnancy. She should have realised that Mrs Avery, as excited about the baby as if it were her own grandchild, and not realising Justin's feelings, had talked to him about her visits to the doctor; she always asked for full reports when Caroline returned home.

When was she going to realise, once and for all, that Justin just didn't care about this child?

'I'm sorry you've been bothered,' she told him bleakly. 'I'll tell her not to worry you with it. But that won't be necessary now, will it?' She looked at him challengingly, her eyes narrowed, her hair a blaze of tumbling curls about her shoulders. She could sense his tension at her question, although not a nerve pulsed to show he was in the least disturbed by it. 'She'll realise you don't care about this pregnancy as soon as I move out and ask her to go with me,' she added at his lack of response.

His hands were thrust into the pockets of his suit trousers. 'And when is that going to be?'

She shrugged, forcing herself to remain calm when what she really longed to do was get up and shake some sense into him, some feeling! 'Tomorrow, I think, don't you?' She looked up at him questioningly, willing him to tell her he didn't want her to go at all. But of course, he didn't.

His breath left his body in a ragged sigh. 'Was it Tony or Sonia who told you about Lindford?'

At least he wasn't attempting to prevaricate about the other man's arrest. 'Does that really matter?' She shook her head. 'I know, and so there's no reason for me to stay on here. Why didn't *you* tell me about him?'

Justin turned away, taking his time about pouring himself a drink.

'Justin!' she finally prompted when she could stand the tension no more.

He turned slowly, a look of utter defeat on his

face, his drink remaining untouched on the side-table. 'Why don't you stay on here until you've found somewhere else to live?'

He wasn't going to say why he hadn't told her about Don Lindford's arrest in America; she could see that by the determined thrust of his jaw. If she weren't so angry with him for his obstinacy she could have cried for what he was so wantonly throwing away. 'I can always stay with my parents for a while,' she said firmly. 'I'm sure they won't mind.'

His mouth twisted into a bitter smile. 'Anything but staying on here!'

'Yes!' Anger flared in her eyes, her struggle to stand up most undignified; Sonia had been right about the crane! Finally she managed to stand across the room from Justin. 'The way things are, I can't stay here!'

He sighed. 'I wish I could say things will change——'

'But you can't,' she finished dismissively, walking to the door.

'Where are you going?' he called out to her.

She stopped, but she didn't turn, too aware of the tears burning to be shed, of too many wasted tears, to put either of them through that again. 'I've already packed my things,' she told him softly. 'I think it would be best if I went to my parents tonight——'

'Don't go!'

She closed her eyes as the pain of parting from him ripped through her. 'Please don't make this any harder than it already is!' she groaned, taking another step out of his life.

'For God's sake, don't go, Caroline!' He stood behind her now, spinning her round to face him, his hands painful on her arms. 'Don't leave me!'

She gazed up at him searchingly, at the pain etched into his face, pride and arrogance stripped from him in this moment of pleading. He was hurting just as badly as she was, but she dared not allow even that to change her mind about leaving. They couldn't go on without love between them, a shared love, a love that included Justin caring for his child.

She shook her head. 'I'm sorry, Justin—oh, don't!' she choked as a silver-wet trail fell unheeded down his grooved cheek at her refusal. 'Oh, my darling, no!' she groaned as she wiped the wetness away with her fingertips, only to find his cheek was instantly wet again, the patch over his unsighted eye rapidly dampening, too. 'Justin, don't!' Her arms were about his waist as she pressed her cheek against his heaving chest.

He held her fiercely to him, his body racked by sobs. 'I love you, Caroline,' he rasped. 'Dear God, how I love you! Don't leave me,' he begged again. 'I'll do anything, anything you want, but don't leave me!'

It broke her heart anew to know that she had done this to him, reduced him to this. But what of their child? As if aware of her thoughts the baby moved impatiently inside her, indignant at the way it was being squashed between their two bodies.

Justin drew back with a pained gasp at the fleeting movement, staring down at the swell of their child, his gaze widening incredulously as he saw an elbow or a knee move against the smoothness of Caroline's dress. He swallowed convulsively, one hand moving tentatively towards her, barely resting against the tautness of her body, but nevertheless receiving a healthy kick in response to his touch.

He looked up at Caroline in wonder, his hand more firmly against her now, feeling the strong movements of his child.

Caroline could see the battle he was fighting with himself, and stood utterly still, barely able to breathe as she waited for the outcome. Since that first time, the baby's movements had grown stronger and more frequent, but she had never again mentioned it to Justin, accepting his lack of interest. But the expression on his face now told her that he hadn't been uninterested at all, that he had been—afraid! Strange as it was, unbelievable as it seemed, she could see the naked fear in his silver gaze.

'Justin?' she prompted dazedly.

He fell to his knees in front of her, his face buried against the child as it nestled so snugly within her. 'She thought I didn't care either.' His voice was muffled against her body. 'She thought because I—because I couldn't cry, that I hadn't loved them. Or her. I wanted to cry,' he choked, fresh tears on the hardness of his cheeks, 'but somehow until I saw you were going to leave, too, I couldn't seem to! I never wanted to hurt her, Caroline,' he told her raggedly. 'I never wanted her to do *that!*'

His words were too disjointed for her to know exactly what he was talking about, but she did understand that he was crying now as if he would never be able to stop. And they were cleansing tears. How she loved him; God, how she loved him! They would work something out for their future so that they could be together; they *had* to.

'Tell me, Justin.' She smoothed the hair back from his sweat-dampened face, dislodging the eye-patch in the process, gasping slightly as Justin reached up to rip it off completely to throw it across the room, leaving himself completely vulnerable.

'This is what I am, Caroline,' he choked. 'Scarred inside and out!'

'Tell me, my love,' she encouraged again, sitting down on the sofa, Justin at her side as she cradled his head against her shoulder. 'I love you,' she reassured him softly.

He drew in a ragged breath. 'Penny and I were both twenty-two when we got married. I—I had wanted to wait before having children, but—we took risks.' He shrugged. 'And within six months of being married Penny was pregnant. She was only three months along when—when she lost it——'

'Oh, Justin . . .' She closed her eyes in pained denial, only now beginning to realise what he had suffered in the past.

He shook his head. 'The baby had barely begun to seem real to me when—when it was gone again,' he said harshly. 'I was upset, naturally I was, but Penny was devastated. It hadn't been a planned baby, but as soon as the doctor declared her fit enough Penny wanted to try again.' He gave a ragged sigh. 'I wasn't so sure. The last time had—well, it had frightened me, and this time I was afraid I might lose Penny, too. But she was ecstatic when she found out she was pregnant again, began to plan the nursery straight away, buying things for the baby, as if doing so would ensure nothing went wrong this time. She had the nursery decorated and ready for occupation by the time she was five months along,' he remembered dully. 'I tried to tell her she should wait, that it would be best to wait until—until we were sure everything was going to be all right. But by the time she reached her fifth month I had begun to hope, too. At night we would—I used to lie beside her waiting for the movements of the baby, and then Penny and I would laugh at how strong he was.' He swallowed hard, lost in the memories.

It was all becoming clear now: Justin's knowledge of pregnancy, of pregnant women, when he had supposedly never had anything to do with them, didn't *want* anything to do with them. Why hadn't she realised that earlier?

'Penny used to call him our little cub.'

As Tony had that night Justin had spilt his champagne, and she had thought it might be because he didn't want to drink a toast to their baby!

That had also been the night he had first dreamt

of Penny, the first time he hadn't made love to *her*. But she could see even that differently now, knew how disturbed he had been about learning of Don Lindford's visit, could see that his distraction had been because he had been worried about her, and that worry had brought forward his nightmares of losing Penny. It even explained his sudden desire for them to go away on a honeymoon; he had been afraid for her when the other man came back. What a fool she had been!

'Penny was just over five months along when the premature labour began,' Justin continued flatly. 'They tried to stop it, but nothing could be done. Our son was too small to survive, as small as one of my hands,' he remembered emotionally. 'They let us see him, and he—he was perfect in every way, except that he was too small!' He shook his head, closing his eyes, his cheeks wet once more. 'Damn it, why couldn't I have cried then!' he groaned forcefully.

'They told Penny she shouldn't risk having any more babies, that more pregnancies would probably end up the same way. Penny begged me to share her pain, for that, and for the babies we had lost, but somehow it was all locked up inside of me and I couldn't let it out. Instead I buried myself in my work. And then one day, I—I came home from work to find Penny in the nursery she refused to redecorate, a bottle of sleeping pills at her side.' He spoke distantly. 'I've often wondered if things might have been different if I just could have cried!'

It was all so obvious now: Justin's reluctance to love, his decision not to have children; to the extent that he had taken the necessary step to ensure that he never did, his lack of interest in their child once he knew he hadn't succeeded. He had been afraid to love this child in case it were taken from him, too. She should have made him talk to her earlier, could have shared the pain and anxiety he couldn't even acknowledge. All those disjointed incidents, Justin's vasectomy, his comment that children were too vulnerable to love, his refusal to accept her pregnancy; they would all have made sense if she had only sat down and thought about them logically, instead of assuming he was still in love with his first wife.

'Justin.' She touched his face tenderly. 'I'm thirty weeks along now; even if I went into labour there's a very good chance they could save the baby. You do want it?' she probed gently.

His eyes darkened. 'That was something else I felt guilty about. I really wanted this child, right from the moment you told me you were pregnant and I first began to hope it could be mine. I loved Penny, but our babies never quite seemed this real to me.' He frowned.

'Possibly because you were too young to appreciate the miracle of them,' Caroline comforted. 'Also this child——' she put his hand against her again, a lump in her throat at the tender fascination on his face '—this child seemed an impossibility to you.'

'*You* seemed an impossibility to me,' he

admitted gruffly. 'After Penny I shut love out of my life, and for twelve years I succeeded. But the first time I looked at you I felt a jolt right where my heart should be. I cold-bloodedly decided it was lust raising its ugly head, and I've learnt that the best way to deal with that is to let it take its course. But you wouldn't let it.' He frowned. 'You were determined to remain faithful to Tony, wouldn't even accept my invitation for dinner until after you had an argument with him. By that time it was more than lust—maybe it always had been,' he acknowledged ruefully. 'Once I had made love to you I knew I couldn't let you go, that I had to hang on to you any way that I could. Even if it meant marrying you. I had no right marrying you believing I was sterile, probably had no right marrying you at all.' He shook his head. 'The night you told me you were pregnant I almost collapsed. Then I began to hope for a miracle. And when that miracle became a reality I was so damned scared I couldn't think straight. What if we lost this baby, too? What if I lost you?' His face was haunted. 'It seemed that if I rejected the baby, ignored its existence, then I didn't have to acknowledge that anything could go wrong.' He gave a bitter smile. 'You see what a coward you've married.'

A coward wouldn't have survived losing the babies and Penny the way that he had, and she knew beyond a shadow of a doubt that it hadn't been because he was cold and unfeeling; that he had loved his wife and children very much. If anything, Justin felt things too deeply, and because he knew how badly he could be hurt he locked his emotions away inside himself and refused to let them out, conquering them instead of letting them defeat him.

Allowing himself to love her meant he could no longer do that, but with the vulnerability had come a chance for a new happiness for him. She would make sure he never knew anything else.

'Our child doesn't think you're a coward, and neither do I.' She looked at him with all the love she had for him showing in her over-bright eyes.

He gave a low groan at her unquestioning acceptance of him. 'That night Sonia told Tony she would be shouting it from the rooftops if she were pregnant with his child I felt so damned guilty for denying you that pride in our child.'

'It doesn't matter,' she assured him huskily. 'The night the baby is born, *you* can go and shout it from the rooftops. Whatever happens, Justin,' she told him warmly as his eyes once again became shadowed at the thought of her having the baby. 'We'll get through it together, because we love each other.'

He looked at her uncertainly. 'You aren't leaving?' he said hesitantly.

'Never,' she promised with feeling. 'Never, never, *never!*' She threw herself into his arms.

She had been wrong that day she denied that pain could be good; the pain Justin had allowed to flow today had cleansed his heart and soul. They could only go forward from here, would look to the future and not the past. And she would give him a healthy child, someone else to fill the great capacity he had for love.

'Darling, what are you doing?'

Justin chuckled against her nape. 'Well, if you don't know I must have been doing it wrong all these years!'

Caroline turned slightly to return the intimacy of his smile, her back arching as his lips moved lower, travelling the length of her spine where he had unzipped the gown she had just put on. 'I thought we were going out for lunch,' she reminded him faintly, Justin's touch inciting its usual magic; lunch was the last thing she felt in the mood for now.

'I didn't say that,' he murmured softly, his fingers playing lightly at the base of her spine. 'I merely asked Sonia and Tony if they would take the children for lunch so that we could celebrate alone.'

She turned in his arms, her hands linked behind his head, nuzzling against his hair-roughened chest, damp still from where he had just taken a shower. 'I assumed we were going out for an anniversary lunch.' She could hear the accelerated beat of his heart, feel his desire against her.

'I intend having a feast.' His tone left no doubt as to who he intended feasting on!

She laughed softly. Four years of marriage hadn't changed their instant awareness of each other, even their children not doing that: their beloved first-born Katy, two-year-old and already independent Aaron, who was so much like his father, and adorable six-month-old James. All the children openly adored their father, and Justin couldn't have been a more gentle or caring parent, especially so because he knew what he had already lost. The night Katy had been born they had both cried with happiness, and their wonder and delight in their children hadn't lessened over the years.

Sonia and Tony expected their first baby in five months' time, and Caroline had a feeling that taking Katy, Aaron, and James for lunch today was their way of seeing how they were going to cope as parents. Knowing her mischievous trio, she had a feeling the other couple might wonder what they had let themselves in for with approaching parenthood by the time they picked the children up in a couple of hours!

The last three and a half years had been happier than Caroline had ever imagined they could be, filled with love and laughter, and most of all with knowing how important she and Justin were to each other, no longer any secrets or shadows between them. Although she would never have wished for it to happen that way, the last remaining shadow to their untroubled happiness had been removed three years ago when Don Lindford had been killed during a knife fight with another prisoner. She hated all kinds of violence, but she loved Justin and her family too much to be genuinely sorry that the man wouldn't be able to come back and threaten them once again.

She now had no doubts as to what her destiny

was to be: unimagined happiness with Justin and their children, for the rest of their lives.

As her gown fell softly to the carpeted floor, she knew she and Justin were fated to be destiny's lovers, for eternity . . .

Harlequin Presents

Coming Next Month

Available in September wherever paperback books are sold, or through Harlequin Reader Service:

In the U.S.
901 Fuhrmann Blvd.
P.O. Box 1397
Buffalo, N.Y. 14240-1397

In Canada
P.O. Box 603
Fort Erie, Ontario
L2A 5X3

ATTRACTIVE, SPACE SAVING BOOK RACK

Display your most prized novels on this handsome and sturdy book rack. The hand-rubbed walnut finish will blend into your library decor with quiet elegance, providing a practical organizer for your favorite hard-or soft-covered books.

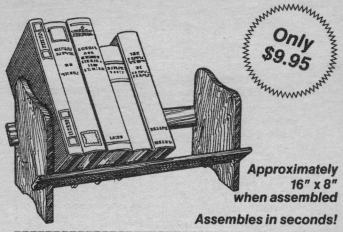

Only $9.95

Approximately 16" x 8" when assembled

Assembles in seconds!

To order, rush your name, address and zip code, along with a check or money order for $10.70* ($9.95 plus 75¢ postage and handling) payable to *Harlequin Reader Service*:

> Harlequin Reader Service
> Book Rack Offer
> 901 Fuhrmann Blvd.
> P.O. Box 1396
> Buffalo, NY 14269-1396
>
> *Offer not available in Canada.*

*New York and Iowa residents add appropriate sales tax.

BKR-1A

Can you keep a secret?

You can keep this one plus 4 free novels

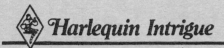

Harlequin American Romance

Romances that go one step farther...
American Romance

Realistic stories involving people you can relate to and care about.

Compelling relationships between the mature men and women of today's world.

Romances that capture the core of genuine emotions between a man and a woman.

Join us each month for four new titles wherever paperback books are sold.
Enter the world of American Romance.
